THE ATLANTIS RIDDLE

KEVIN TUMLINSON

PROLOGUE

WEST ORANGE, NEW JERSEY—DECEMBER 10, 1914

THOMAS EDISON STOOD ON THE LAWN OF HIS WEST Orange laboratory and watched the buildings burn.

All around him he heard the sounds of the fire brigade—bells clanging, horses clomping as they brought wagons of water and men to the site. There were even some of Ford's automobiles racing forward, skidding to a stop so that men could rush out and add their hands to help fight the blaze.

Edison didn't look at them, but instead watched as his life's work literally went up in smoke. Ten buildings filled with his patents, his research, his prototypes, and his finished inventions—the work that he and his people had labored over for decades would soon be only so much ash.

He smiled, and even chuckled to himself a bit.

Local people were gathering now, of course, shuffling out of their homes or places of business. A great number were his own employees—many of whom had been busy working when the klaxons sounded and they were forced to rush outside. Those that had homes close by eventually gathered with their families, if they had them. The rest either rushed to help put out the fire or stood aside gawking in disbelief. Some even wept.

Charlie Edison stood not far from his father, amid a cluster of workers and neighbors. He looked so distraught that it almost made Edison burst out laughing. Edison made his way to Charlie, and when he reached him he said, "Go get your mother and her friends! They'll never see a fire like this again!"

Charlie looked at him, half dazed. "Poppa, it's all burning! All of your work!"

Edison smiled and shook his head, waving dismissively toward the ten burning buildings. "It's alright," Edison said. "We've just got rid of a lot of rubbish."

Charlie stared at his father, shaking his head unconsciously. Edison knew what his son was thinking. His old man had lost his mind. His life's work burned right in front of him, and Edison stood and watched with a smile on his face. What would this mean to the business? What would it mean to the employees and their families? What would it mean to Edison himself?

Edison planned to answer those questions. He knew, as surely as he knew his own name, that *they* would come. And soon. The press would be there, as they had *always* been there.

Edison didn't mind. He actually liked the press. He'd figured them out years ago. He knew that if he gave them a good enough show, they'd lap it up and print just about anything he wanted. He could control every word of their stories, just by being a good showman. He'd done it most of his career. He was a master at it.

Charlie did as he was told, running to fetch his mother and her friends. They would come and gawk and whisper to each other, telling themselves stories of how Edison brought this disaster upon himself, with all of his 'research and scientific study.' They would say this was his great fall. They would imply that it had been inevitable. He was trying to accomplish too much, to fly too high, they'd say. His wings were made of wax, and now he'd finally gone too close to the sun.

That made Edison smile even more.

Because he knew a secret.

He had *started* this fire.

No one else would ever know the truth of it. He would allow the stories to run rampant, allow the gossip to take root wherever it could. He would say nothing to correct the record. All these people, these lookers-on, would cover what he'd done better than any story he could concoct himself.

He had insured the place, of course. But the money would barely scratch the surface. By his own estimate, Edison figured he'd just burned up nearly a million dollars in research and materials and equipment. All of his records, all of the test materials he and his employees had gathered, over decades of research—all gone. The insurance might cover a third of the damage, if that much.

But it was worth it.

Hours later, when the buildings were just heaps of cinder and ash, Edison stood in a cleared circle, with people gathered all about. He looked at the gaggle of reporters as they stood impatiently, chomping, waiting for him to throw them their meat. And so he did.

Someone had produced an apple crate, and Edison stood on this like a stage. He put his hands in his pockets, which he knew made him look relaxed, confident, unfazed.

He told the reporters that it might appear to be a sad day, but the reality was this was a rare *opportunity*. He told them that much had been lost, but the real treasures were still alive. The thoughts and memories and ideas were still there, even without his lab. He told them he was exhausted from being here until the very end, until the last drop of water left the brigade's buckets, and the last flame flickered out. But he left them with one abiding message.

"Although I am over 67 years old," he stated, "I will start over again tomorrow."

That simple statement prompted cheers from his own employees, as well as from the crowds of citizens, and even the reporters themselves. Everyone loved a hero, especially one of legendary proportions. And Edison had done much to make himself legendary, in his time.

It was true, too. He *would* start again. In fact, the next morning, after taking one of his customary naps, Edison oversaw the start of rebuilding the facility. He directed workers to start using fresh materials as well as salvaged materials, to build new spaces for the work to continue. No one questioned the fact that both workers and materials were already in place and ready to go. This was Edison—*the Wizard of Menlo Park*. He had but to wave his hand, and such things appeared.

No one would ever guess or know that he had arranged for all of this in advance. He could start at daybreak the next morning because he had planned to start then anyway.

He stood right at the edge of the construction zone when the men began their work. He watched as they cleared the ash and ruins of the old and started building the new. They retrieved a few things from the ruins, and Edison was glad of it. But none of that really mattered. The only thing he actually cared about had been removed before the fire had even begun.

In fact, his most prized possession rested in the pocket of his coat right this very minute.

He slipped a hand in his pocket and felt it there. The weight of it was comforting. Solid.

In his travels and research and study, he had never

encountered an artifact quite like this one. But it had changed *everything* for him.

A small, triangular shaped bit of stone, almost the size of his palm. It had various markings engraved in its surface, with fine threads of gold weaving patterns he was only just starting to understand—a language lost to history, translatable only in fragments so far.

Along its edges were grooves, indicating that this was a piece of a larger object—a second half. Edison had studied that stone, too, and had separated the two halves so that only he could have access to what the two stones could unlock together. These stones had given more to the world than anyone would ever know. And there was more on the way.

There were hints of something *bigger*. Something *ancient*. All Edison had to do was prepare and study.

He'd already learned so much. Many of his inventions had come as a result of studying this one artifact, and following where it had led him. Much of his life's work— along with all the fame and all the accolades and all the wealth—could be traced back to this little triangle of stone and its mate across the sea. Though no one in the world, not even his family, knew of either stone's existence.

If he was the Wizard of Menlo Park, then this was his *Philosopher's Stone.*

But his next great achievement would make him more than just a Wizard. What he planned to do next would make him a Master of History.

Edison knew that all great leaps forward required 'burning the nest.' Like the legendary phoenix, in order to be born new, to gain true power, one had to lay all of the past in ash and cinder. There was a power in wiping the slate clean and starting again—in turning your back on the past and starting on a new path. There was power in rebirth.

That's what this was. This little exercise was the crucible

that would purify Edison and his employees. It would be a rallying cry. It would get them on track for something bigger than they had managed to accomplish so far. Bigger than light bulbs and batteries and phonographs. Bigger than anything his men had been working on before the fire.

There had been too many lines of pursuit. He knew that. He'd known it for quite some time. Their focus had been too split, and so they were less effective than they could have been.

But what he'd built here—it had been *unstoppable*. It had too much momentum for even Edison himself to put on the brakes. Unless, of course, he was willing to destroy it all for this new cause.

And he was.

As the crews arrived and the work started in earnest, Edison busied himself with directing his foremen and the crews. He prioritized their workload. And he oversaw reclamation. Anything that was found in the rubble which was still viable, Edison wanted transferred to a location miles away. "To be sorted later," Edison said. Much of it, he knew, would never see the light of day again. Not in his lifetime, at least. But the nostalgic part of him wanted to hold on to all of it—reminders of who he'd come to be here.

He directed the crews to clear the rubble, but before they began rebuilding he added an addition. He fancied one of Ford's automobiles, he said, and an invention so fine needed a good home. "We'll build a garage," he said. "And we will make it usable as a workspace as well." He handed the foreman onsite a blueprint—one which he himself had drafted. It detailed exactly what Edison wanted, including some non-standard items. The foreman was a man Edison had dealt with many times in the past, and he was used to some of Edison's eccentricities. He never questioned a thing, but instead got his men to work on the task of digging and laying foundations.

Edison watched that work for a time, and went on to direct the rest of the rebuilding.

This was the fresh start he needed. It was the first step on the road to something so big, so monumental, that it had been spoken about as far back as Plato, in his works *Timaeus* and *Critias*—works that most assumed to be wholly allegorical.

What Edison had in his coat pocket, however, was something far from allegory. It was *proof*. It was a *key*. It was part of a larger map that would point, inevitably, to a lost civilization, and all of the science and technology that was buried with it.

From these ashes, Edison thought, *a new world will rise from the old*. He smiled at the poetry of it, and then busied himself with the task of rebuilding his labs, so that he could start reshaping the world.

LAOS, 60 MILES EAST OF CHAVAN—SEPTEMBER 13, 1974

They weren't supposed to be here. That's what made this all the more tricky.

Technically, the US had no presence or jurisdiction in Laos. US troops were never to set foot 'over the fence.' The hot territory was Vietnam, and that's where Captain McCarthy and his SOG team were meant to stay.

But orders were orders.

Their mission was interference. Pull attention away from another operation, happening about fifty klicks to the West of their current position. And for three days, that's exactly the play they ran. For more than 72 hours now, McCarthy and his men had dodged and fired and crawled their way through dense jungle, fighting an enemy that surrounded them on every side, defending a big patch of nothing at all, while another team ran a more targeted and clandestine operation somewhere to the West. Their only job—keep the enemy occupied while this other team made easy ingress and got out again with less than a scratch.

And it worked.

McCarthy led 16 Army special forces operatives, plus a few hundred Montagnard mercenaries, straight up the backside of the North Vietnamese. And he'd made it hurt.

For three days they had taken on the enemy right on their home turf, and in the end it had required calling in an airstrike to lift them out. Three Sikorsky CH-53 helicopters and a number of fixed-wing aircraft had performed a shocking number of strafing runs and dodges through live fire, with the birds dropping in to pick up McCarthy's men in groups. The injured went out first, and one CH-53 was dropped by enemy fire before everyone was out of the hot zone.

To everyone's surprise, not one American soldier died on the mission. Three of McCarthy's Montagnards had taken fatal hits—something that McCarthy mourned over right alongside their compatriots. But considering the level of threat, and the odds against them, this mission went off as smooth as butter.

Operation Crosswind was a success.

And in more ways than one.

McCarthy was on one of the last birds to leave the hot zone. Clouds of tear gas wafted among the trees, and in the morning light it looked like a menacing fog. He saw enemy combatants ducking for cover as the fixed-wings laid suppression fire. And he saw the fallen CH-53—now a smoking wreck that was almost unidentifiable. They had hit it with missiles and incendiaries, to prevent the enemy from salvaging it for use against American troops, and its smoldering corpse made for a haunting image that would stick with McCarthy for the rest of his life.

At McCarthy's feet, rumbling and vibrating on the floor of the CH-53, was a footlocker filled with an unexpected treasure.

After three days of fighting their way through the jungle, and just before calling in air strikes and rescue, one of McCarthy's men called in a find. While clearing a spider hole, they came across a cache of documents—maps, communiques, troop orders. It was a *huge* intelligence find, and potentially a tide-turning boon for the Americans. The cache contained information on troop deployment, as well as key locations that would be strike targets soon enough.

But it also contained something else.

McCarthy put a hand in his pocket and felt the little stone triangle there. And with it, the neatly rolled piece of parchment that was a map more ancient than anything McCarthy had ever before seen. It was wrapped in protective plastic, but it still seemed somehow vulnerable to the high humidity of the region. McCarthy didn't know much about antiquities or ancient artifacts, but he knew treasure when he saw it.

They'd been found by Van Burren and his Hatchet force —two odd, out-of-place pieces of ancient history, hidden among the cache of military intelligence.

Van Burren was a slimy bastard—he and McCarthy had a history of static. The man came into the war with money, and a profound sense of entitlement. He had risen in the ranks quickly, and that had just exacerbated his attitude problems. McCarthy didn't like him, didn't trust him, and didn't want him on his team. But orders were orders. And

Van Burren did happen to be good at ferreting out enemy intelligence.

Van Burren was also an expert on antiquities—the product of a wealthy upbringing.

He'd shown McCarthy the map, and the stone. He hadn't had much choice—several members of Van Burren's Hatchet force were extremely loyal to McCarthy, and they'd been there in the moment when Van Burren had opened the foot locker. They'd seen everything that was in there, and it hadn't escaped their notice that an ancient looking map and a stone straight out of *Lord of the Rings* had been right on top of the intelligence cache. McCarthy was going to know about it, either way.

Van Burren had grinned when he handed it over, proud of himself for the find, but also trying to snow McCarthy into believing that, 'aw shucks,' he'd intended to hand this over all along. And he had explained to McCarthy exactly what it was. Or, at least, what he could *interpret* that it was, from the writing on the map.

"The markings on the stone—I have no idea what those mean," Van Burren said. "But the map has some hand-written notes, in pencil. And there are map coordinates on it that I'm pretty sure were not written by our NVA buddies here."

"What's it a map of?" McCarthy had asked.

Van Burren didn't know. "Some island, I think," he had said. "But the real important part is what's *on* that island. The notes talk about gold and other treasures. And a lot of it."

Gold. Of *course* Van Burren was concerned about *gold*. McCarthy wasn't sure he could prove it just yet, but he suspected that Van Burren was using US troops and resources to run drugs, art, artifacts, and anything else he could profit from. Finding a large cache of gold would be a huge windfall for Van Burren. He'd be richer than he was now. Maybe rich

enough to buy his way out of the war, and get back home
with pockets filled with loot.

Meanwhile, McCarthy—the 'old man' of the group, since
he was the only one to have reached 30 years old so far—he'd
be lucky to even survive long enough to see an end to this
conflict. Back home, in North Carolina, the family farm had
been seized by the bank. His father had passed away from a
heart attack while McCarthy had been in-country, probably
from the stress of losing everything. And his mother wasn't
doing so well either—she'd taken ill just after daddy died,
and the neighbors had finally taken her in for care. Hospital
bills were already stacking up. And even with an officer's
bump in pay, if McCarthy managed to leave this jungled hell
alive he'd be in debt for most if not all of his life.

And then there was his wife.

She was young, in her mid-twenties. And she was beautiful. He had married her while he was on leave, and hadn't
regretted it for a minute. When he got back, he planned to
get to the business of making babies with her—that was just
a fact. But what if he couldn't afford to start a family? What
if he couldn't get it together enough to take care of her and
any kids they might have?

There was a thud below McCarthy's feet.

"Just took a lucky pop shot," the gunner shouted to him,
grinning. "Probably not much more than a dimple in
our butt."

McCarthy nodded. And then patted the pocket where
the stone and the map rested. He looked up to see Van
Burren staring at him, watching him as if he was aware of
exactly everything McCarthy was thinking. And then Van
Burren nodded, his features solemn.

The deal had been struck.

McCarthy felt almost like vomiting over it, but there it
was. Of all the men he knew, all the good men he'd led, he

would never have imagined striking up a partnership with *Van Burren*. He was the worst human being McCarthy had ever met. Even the NVA might have been more honorable.

But war makes for odd bedfellows. And so does business. McCarthy was doing something he knew to be illegal and even immoral, so there really were few better partners than Van Burren, when it came to that.

They landed at *Kon Tum* an hour later, and after their debriefing McCarthy and Van Burren slipped off for a beer and a chat—both of which had turned McCarthy's stomach. They made their plans and their deals. They agreed upon their split. And they agreed upon who controlled what, in terms of the map and the artifact. Insurance against each other, as it were.

McCarthy was part of Van Burren's network now. He'd already more or less turned a blind eye to some of what Van Burren was doing—despite being a scumbag, the man was a capable soldier and good at his job. He was a tactical thinker, which made him invaluable in the field. But McCarthy couldn't shake the feeling that he'd made a very one-sided deal with the devil in all of this. And he knew that someday, somehow, the deal would come back to haunt him.

The devil would get his due.

PART 1

CHAPTER 1

MANHATTAN, NEW YORK—DECEMBER 16, 2016

DAN KOTLER WAS TIRED OF THE PRESS.

He knew them all by now—reporters from every major and minor newspaper, from every local affiliate television station, from every blog and vlog and podcast imaginable. The story of the Coelho Medallion, and the presence of Vikings in North America, had been *huge*, and had fired the imagination of everyone. It was still simmering, really, even after all of these months with only minor new discoveries and small revelations. The public was still hopeful, and so the press was still circling.

But enough was enough.

He had walked out of his Upper East Side apartment, and as soon as he spotted a few familiar and eager faces on the sidewalk he turned and walked right back inside. The doorman, Ernest, smiled and nodded to him. "They're back, sir?" he asked.

"They're back," Kotler said.

"Same trick as last time?" Ernest asked.

Kotler grinned and nodded.

Ernest picked a mobile phone from his pocket. He made

a brief call that would have sounded vague and cryptic to anyone but Kotler. And then he nodded to Kotler, extending a hand toward a paneled door behind the little podium where Ernest occasionally sat.

Kotler pushed the door open and stepped into the narrow corridor beyond.

This was a 'servants hall,' though no one would really refer to it that way in this day and age. When the building had originally been constructed it was during a less enlightened time in U.S. history. The place had been a hotel, in it's previous incarnation, and many of the employees lived here full time, below stairs as it were. The basement of the building had been a series of servants quarters connected by a network of tunnels and hallways that provided exits to various key rooms on the ground floor of the hotel. The kitchen, the dining room, the smoking lounge and many other amenities could all be reached from this network, so that the servants and hotel employees could move about without being 'under foot.'

All of those spaces had been renovated when the hotel became an apartment building, but the corridors still led to some interesting places—including a fairly secret exit to a parking garage attached behind the building.

Kotler knew that one of the favorite stories spinning among the press was that he was independently wealthy. The press and the public seemed to get a thrill out of the idea of a 'rich guy' crawling around in caves and tunnels, sifting through dirt, looking for treasure. Some of the more progressive publications liked to paint him as greedy and egotistical —as if he was trying to bloom his wealth further by dipping into antiquities, and then flaunting his brilliance in the press by claiming discoveries he hadn't made all on his own.

Kotler wished he could correct the record on things like that. He wanted to point out that he hadn't *discovered* the

Coelho Medallion, *or* the underground river. He'd been there for completely different reasons, and had become part of the story. He wasn't trying to steal thunder from Dr. Eloi Coelho —the man for whom the medallion had been named. He was only helping to uncover more secrets, more history that had been long forgotten.

Thoughts of Dr. Coelho caused a pang in Kotler's stomach. It had been a couple of weeks since he'd checked in on his old friend. In that time, Coelho had finally been moved back to a hospital, where he was being treated for pneumonia and other complications from the gunshot wound he had suffered. The wound had healed slowly—and in some ways was still healing. Coelho's body wasn't recovering as quickly as it should. It didn't look good.

Kotler determined he would stop by to see the man later in the day. It would be tricky getting there, but worth the effort to see his old friend.

He exited into the parking structure and skirted the grey walls, stepping alternately through pools of artificial light and valleys of gradient darkness. The garage housed hundreds of very expensive cars, property of the tenants of his building, usually driven by a hired driver. Kotler had never had the urge to own a car—that ubiquitous symbol of personal independence for so many adolescents, and the status symbol of choice for so many wealthy individuals. He had enough independence in his ability to move about in the world without serious limits. And he had no desire to display his status. He preferred to let his work do that on his behalf.

But the garage was an exit that tended to go unnoticed or unobserved by the press. He could slip out to the street, where he could call for a cab or an Uber driver. Ernest had cleared his exit with the security desk in the garage, so they would be on the lookout, warning Kotler if any press happened to be outside. He could hang with them in the small office, just inside the garage, and wait for a car to arrive. They'd done this a few times now, and Kotler appreciated their help and their company.

"Dr. Kotler?" a woman's voice said quietly, from just ahead.

Kotler felt his heart thump once and then drop.

They found me.

This little secret exit had been his last hope of relief from the paparazzi, and now it was done. He could report whoever this was, and have them removed from the garage. This was a fairly secure area, actually, and outsiders weren't permitted.

But before he could say something to that effect, the owner of the voice stepped into a pool of light.

She wasn't someone Kotler recognized. Her blonde hair fell in gentle, boutique waves on either side of a blemish-free face. She was wearing a dress that did an absolutely wonderful job of telling the story of her figure—a shape that would be the envy of most super models.

Kotler was far from lecherous, but also far from absolutely virtuous. He appreciated beautiful women, and he had to admit that *this* woman was absolutely breathtaking.

And, he realized, she was standing alone in a darkened parking structure. Calling his name.

"Do we know each other?" Kotler asked. He was suddenly on alert. As attractive as she was, Kotler knew that such things didn't determine character, and they did not limit motives. She might be a distraction, so that someone could take Kotler from behind.

It happened, from time to time. Occupational hazard.

Or she might choose to take him out herself. *That* happened, too. It was a cultural failing to assume that a beautiful woman couldn't also be capable of dangerous acts. He'd allowed that cultural bias to get him into trouble a time or two in the past.

She shook her head. "No. We've never met," she said. "My name is Abigail McCarthy. My friends call me Gail."

Kotler studied her for a moment, reading her. Her body language was tense, stiff. She was agitated. But she wasn't broadcasting a threat. Neither was she broadcasting vulnerability. Whoever she was, and whatever her motives for being here, she had no fear of Kotler, and she presented no threat. She had the bearing of someone who was capable and able to defend herself, but showed no signs of malice toward him.

Kotler couldn't help but smile. "What can I do for you, Gail? You're obviously not with the press."

She laughed, lightly. "No, definitely not. I don't have a good relationship with the press."

"Oh?" Now this piqued Kotler's interest. He didn't recognize this woman, but she must clearly have some level of notoriety.

"Because of my grandfather, mostly," she said. "Edward McCarthy."

Kotler blinked. "Of McCarthy and Van Burren? The real estate giants?"

She nodded, a tight smile on her lips.

"I'm in the presence of local royalty," Kotler smiled. "What can I do for you?"

She looked around at the garage, seeming truly nervous for the first time. She stepped forward again, and this time came close enough to Kotler that she could reach out and offer him something.

Kotler held out a palm, reflexively, and Gail dropped something small, hard, and smooth into his hand. "Do you know what this is?" she asked.

Kotler looked down at his hand. They were standing slightly in the dark, and he could see only the shape of it and hints of some form of engraving. He stepped forward, looking closely. For the first time he noticed the gold filament, the strange symbols that were clearly a language. He also noted that the triangular stone had a series of grooves and protrusions along one side—evidence that it was meant to connect to a separate piece. This was only one piece of a larger whole.

Kotler didn't recognize it, or the symbols carved into it.

He handed it back to Gail, who had a look of subtle disappointment on her face.

"I'm sorry," he said. "It's an interesting piece, but I'm afraid I've never seen anything like it before."

"Never?" she asked, a slight tone of desperation now rising in her voice. "Or anything similar to it?"

Kotler shook his head. "No, I'm sorry."

She sighed, and let her hands drop to her side. "I had hoped you would recognize it. That would have made things easier."

"What is it?" Kotler asked.

She shook her head. "There's too much to explain here. Maybe … maybe we could go for a drive?"

"A drive?" Kotler asked. "Wait, do you live in the building?"

She smiled. "These days, yes," she said. "My grandfather's company recently purchased several apartments here. I stay here from time to time. I knew you lived here, and I thought you might be taking this exit today. I saw the press outside. This is how I get away from them, when they're on my scent. Ernest always arranges it."

Kotler nodded and smiled. "I see. Ernest has been cheating on me with other tenants. Alright, Ms. McCarthy. I'm game. I was planning to visit a friend this afternoon, but most of my day is clear. What say we grab a cup of coffee?"

"I'd like that," she nodded. "And I know just the place."

They sat close to the windows near the front entrance of *Joe Coffee*—a quaint and slightly rustic coffee shop that

Kotler had been to only once before. Gail, it seemed, was a regular—the barista had her cappuccino ready before she'd even placed her order.

Kotler sipped his latte and waited. Gail was back to confident, apparently at home here, despite seeming a bit out of place. "My grandfather loved this place," she said, glancing around and smiling. "One of the offices is near here. The one he liked to work from most."

"I heard he and Van Burren tried to work as far apart from each other as possible at all times," Kotler said.

Gail smiled lightly. "It's true. They weren't really friends. Just business partners. They met when Van Burren served with my grandfather in Vietnam."

Kotler nodded.

In fact, as he'd read it, Van Burren had been under McCarthy's command during the conflict. They'd come out of the army together, both having served in SOG—the military's 'Studies and Observation Group.' They were a special forces unit that ran clandestine operations, often in direct opposition to international treaty. McCarthy and Van Burren had both been featured in a CNN story that had broken in the '90s, accusing Van Burren in particular of running an underground smuggling operation that moved everything from drugs to antiquities across international borders. Van Burren was suspected of black market ties, but nothing ever seemed to stick.

The smuggling was why Kotler had paid close attention. Smugglers had moved a great many cultural artifacts out of Vietnam and Laos during the war. Much of it had never been recovered. All of it hinted at volumes of history that Kotler would have loved to study. Thanks to the actions of men like Van Burren, however, it was extremely difficult to get clearance to visit ruins and sites in North Vietnam. American researchers tended to disappear in the harsh jungles, which were rumored to still harbor isolated people who were apparently unaware that the war was long over.

Maybe they were right. The United States continued to conduct operations in the region for decades after the Vietnam conflict. For all Kotler or anyone else knew, the war might still be running strong there.

"So," Kotler said after a moment and a sip of latte. "What is it you'd like to tell me, Ms. McCarthy?"

"Please, call me Gail," she said. "And it's a very long story. One that has details I'm not actually all that sure about. But I've followed your career lately." She smirked. "A lot of people have, I know. Vikings in America? Very exciting."

"For a while," Kotler said, smiling. "Eventually it's just another research site, or another piece of ship debris. There are crews still finding artifacts, and there have been some exciting new insights. Divers have dredged up all sorts of interesting artifacts from the bottom of the river, and they're remarkably well preserved. It's still a productive site. But I think I've done as much there as I'm able. I've moved on."

"To what, if I may ask?" Gail said.

Kotler shrugged. "I have several ongoing research projects. Lectures. Appearances. A couple of books I need to finish and hand to my editor."

"Sounds tedious," Gail said.

Kotler liked the way her lips pressed together—as if she were teasing him a bit, trying to get him to confess he was bored with his life at the moment.

He wasn't. Not really.

He'd just come to that point in the research where he felt he'd already contributed as much as he could. His particular skill set could be better used elsewhere. He just hadn't found that 'right project' yet. It was hard to move from something with as high a profile as the Coelho dig site into something as 'mundane' as brushing dust from pieces of broken pottery.

And, of course, there were his academic colleagues. Lately, he'd received more than his usual snubbing from certain professionals in the field. There was resentment— Kotler was an independent, and some felt that he had unfair advantages in that he could fund his own work, and had no university or departmental restrictions to adhere to.

The most recent affront came when he submitted a paper about the Coelho site for peer review, and the entire panel rejected it without so much as cracking the cover. Kotler might not need the approval of the academic community to do his work, but he certainly appreciated having it. He thought of them all as colleagues—brothers-in-arms. It was becoming clear that he was mistaken. He was, and might always be, the outsider.

He shook his head slightly, clearing away the growing feeling of unrest regarding his career. He would find some sort of resolution. Later. Eventually. For now, though, maybe there was another riddle he could help to solve.

"The ... well, the stone you have," Kotler said. "You were hoping I recognized it. Why?"

She shook her head. "Something my grandfather mentioned about you once," she said.

"I had no idea your grandfather would have thought of me at all," Kotler said. "I don't believe he and I have met yet."

Suddenly her features changed, and sadness melted away the imp-like smirk and the troublemaker twinkle in her eye. Kotler knew instantly why.

"When did your grandfather pass?" he asked.

She sniffed and wiped at her eyes with a paper napkin. The Joe Coffee logo looked incongruous in her perfectly manicured hand. "About a week ago," she said. "Lung cancer."

"I'm very sorry," Kotler said. He reached a hand out and placed it on hers, and she accepted it.

"We knew it was coming," she said. "We've been working on getting the company ready for a transition in leadership. His estate was cared for. Everything was taken care of, actually."

"Will you take over his position with the company?" Kotler asked.

She shook her head. "I don't want that. I was never that heavily involved in the actual day-to-day operations, and I don't feel it would be right to use my relationship with Grandad to take over. When my father died, I started working with Grandad just to help out, to have something to do. I was never all that interested in real estate. So Van Burren has stepped up as CEO, and one of the Presidents will take Van Burren's place as COO."

Kotler nodded. "I had no idea. I've been a bit preoccupied lately. I haven't been paying much attention to the news."

She laughed lightly. "That's because you *are* the news," she said.

Kotler shrugged. There was no point denying that. And as much as he was wanting to avoid the press now, he had to admit to having played to them for awhile. He'd done it largely in the hope that publicity would lead to more funding for the dig, so that he could know it could keep going without assistance.

But if he was being honest, his ego hadn't minded the attention either. For a time, at least. He was not above enjoying recognition for his accomplishments. He just preferred that they actually *be* his accomplishments. The ambiguous nature of the Coelho find was uncomfortable to Kotler. It was part of why he wanted to move on, so that the hard working people making all the discoveries could also get the benefit of fame and praise.

So far, though, distancing himself from the project was leaving a hole to fill.

Gail reached into her purse and took out a smartphone. She tapped the screen for a moment, then slid it across to Kotler.

On the screen was a photo of the triangular stone he'd seen earlier. Only something was off. "Is this image flipped?" he asked. "The ridges are on the opposite side." He looked closer. "No," he said. "This is a *different* stone. Is it the mate?"

He looked up and Gail nodded. "I think so," she said.

"Think?" Kotler asked. "You don't have it?"

She shook her head. "No. In fact, that image represents the only evidence I've ever found that it even exists. My grandfather and I spent millions on private investigators, searching for it. That photo comes from an insurance inventory. It's supposed to be private, so I haven't pressed the investigator on how he was able to procure a copy, but the stone itself hasn't been seen in decades."

"So what is it?" Kotler asked. "It's clearly very old. The gold filament is tarnished, which doesn't tell me much, but the inlay is something akin to what the ancient Egyptians used. And I've never seen the patterns."

"We think it's a language. I mean … my *grandfather* and I thought it was a language. Something that hasn't existed for thousands of years."

"A dead language?" Kotler asked. "From what region?"

"At first we thought Asia," Gail said. "But now we're not so certain. Grandad thought it might have come from the Mediterranean, maybe some offshoot of Greek, but that was disproven eventually. Our experts put it 'somewhere in between,' usually."

"Ok," Kotler said. He handed the phone back to Gail. "So I'm at a loss here."

She smiled lightly, then took a deep breath. "The stone I

showed you earlier—that was part of the estate my grandfather left me. Van Burren has been pressuring me to hand it over since I got my hands on it, but so far I'm not under any legal obligation to do that."

"So far?" Kotler asked.

She shook her head, and her body language instantly shifted. She was annoyed, even angry. "He has the company's lawyers combing my grandfather's will, trying to find any loopholes or errors. He claims they were 50/50 owners of this thing. That it should have gone to him when my grandfather died, and it wasn't eligible to be part of his estate. And all of that may be true, for all I know. But …"

She hesitated, staring out of the window at a large panel truck passing by.

"But it was your grandfather's," Kotler said. "And something the two of you shared."

She looked at him, a slightly surprised expression on her face. "That," she said. "Yes. But also, I think my grandfather … well he didn't *trust* Van Burren. That was public knowledge. But this went deeper somehow. He specifically left me this stone, with instructions that I was to keep it safe from Van Burren."

"Keep it safe?" Kotler asked. He shook his head, then sipped his latte. When he placed the ceramic cup back on the table he said, "I think you'd better fill me in on everything. It sounds like you need some help. Or at least some advice. And I'm working from very little knowledge here."

Gail nodded, her hands slowly spinning the cup of cappuccino on the table top as she thought, and then spoke.

"My grandfather was Van Burren's commanding officer in Vietnam. He told me about a mission—almost fifty years ago. It was a big deal. Something secret at the time. A distraction, meant to pull attention away from a bigger operation. Grandad and his men managed to get through a pretty rough few days, with the enemy constantly surrounding them. And then Van Burren found this intelligence cache. A locker filled with documents. But also a few antiquities. Pieces that at first they thought were part of Laotian culture. They later found out it was something else—brought in from a distant land, back when the Degar—the indigenous people of Vietnam—still had control of the country."

"Degar ... the Montagnards?" Kotler asked.

Gail nodded.

The term 'Montagnard' was French for 'mountain people,' which described the Degar perfectly. Originally their population occupied the costal regions, but invasions by the Vietnamese and Cambodians had forced them into the mountains, where they quickly adapted and flourished. During the Vietnam conflict, many Montagnards served as mercenary forces, largely assisting US soldiers in combat, supplying valuable intel into the lay of the land, and the activities of the North Vietnamese.

The US lost the conflict in Vietnam, but the losses would have been much greater and the conflict would have been much more devastating if not for the assistance of the Montagnards. And today they were nearly an extinct race.

Numerous Montagnards were transplanted from Vietnam to various regions around the world, for their own safety. Kotler had actually been to a Montagnard settlement right here in the US, in North Carolina, and had studied the ongoing culture of these people. It broke his heart to see them, exiled from their own lands, but it gave him hope that despite their exile they were *flourishing*. They were a hearty people, and highly adaptable—Kotler deeply admired them.

"Grandad commanded hundreds of Montagnards mercenaries during this mission. They made it possible for the Americans to stay alive for three days with enemy on all sides. A few of them died fighting for us, and Grandad always honored them on the same day every year. It was a family tradition, and one I never really questioned until I was old enough to hear the stories."

"So on this mission," Kotler said, "you're saying that the stone you have was found among the cache of enemy intelligence?"

Gail nodded. "Grandad said Van Burren found it, and because there were other soldiers and Montagnards with him, he had no choice but to admit to it and hand the stone over. There was also a map—an old map, with some hand written notes. Van Burren has that."

"Did they discover where the map led?" Kotler asked.

"Van Burren must have," she said. "Because he … well, he came back to the US with a lot of gold and other valuables. He used his black market smuggling network in Vietnam to get everything to the US, usually in caskets."

Kotler nodded. It became a common practice, at one point, for smugglers like Van Burren to use caskets to transport contraband. After all, there were plenty of them, and they were rarely searched.

No customs. No reporting. If Van Burren had people in place stateside, he could easily have moved millions of dollars in art, culture artifacts, drugs, weapons, and God knew what else.

"Dad let him get away with the smuggling," Gail said. "He wasn't proud of it. But he told me once that he would have done it again, since it meant that grandmother was taken care of. When they had my father, he felt like he had to keep things going. He wanted to provide his children with the kind of life he never had. And he did. So he let Van Burren get away with his smuggling operation right up until the end of the conflict."

"And by that point he was in business with Van Burren," Kotler said.

"They were in business from the moment Van Burren found that stone. Grandad made Van Burren's life a lot easier —opening up channels for him that he didn't quite have access to. Van Burren was already somewhat rich when he went into the military, mostly from his family's money. But now he was wealthy from his own efforts, and he liked it. And he got Grandad so mired in it that there was no way out."

"Tell me about the artifact," Kotler said. "And why you wanted me to see it."

Gail glanced around the coffee shop, sipped her cappuccino, and then stared out of the window. "When Van Burren and my grandfather came back to the United States, they almost immediately left again. Before she died, my grandmother told me she had been surprised by that. Grandad hadn't been home more than a few months before he was flying out again, this time on private planes, right back to Cambodia. He told me later that they were following leads they'd found on the stone. They were searching for a city— the place where this stone had been found, originally."

"Did they find it?" Kotler asked.

"They thought so," she said. "But no. They found another city altogether, and one that someone else had reached first. It was a ruin. I've seen photos. Grandaddy and Van Burren searched it from end to end, with a team of mercenaries and contractors. They found a few items, but not what they were looking for."

"What were they looking for?" Kotler asked.

She laughed. "You're going to think it's crazy."

"I think everything in this world is crazy," Kotler smiled. "That's why I love it."

She shook her head, smiling. "They were looking for Atlantis."

Kotler arched his eyebrows and laughed. "Now *that's*

unexpected. They thought they would find Atlantis in *Cambodia?*"

"Mostly they were looking for hints to its location, and they were retracing the steps of whoever created the map and found the stone. The map they found had some scrawled notes on it, and those included coordinates and descriptions of a lost city in Cambodia. The notes were actually written in English."

"English? So the map was lifted from someone. A solider, maybe?"

Gail shook her head. "Grandad never knew for sure how the map and the stone came to be in that footlocker, but he and Van Burren did discover one fact. That map had once belonged to Thomas Edison. And those notes were in his handwriting."

Kotler had been mid-sip on his latte when Gail mentioned Edison, and he'd nearly choked. He recovered, wiping his mouth with a napkin and staring at her. "As in *the* Thomas Edison? Inventor? Genius?"

She nodded.

"What …" Kotler started, then shook his head. "What in the world was he doing with a map to a lost city in *Cambodia?*" But Kotler held up a hand before Gail could answer. "No, actually, that's right up his alley. Edison was constantly on the search for new ideas and useful materials, all over the planet. It shouldn't surprise me at all that he made his way to Cambodia at some point. So Edison made the map?"

"It's older than that," Gail said. "*Really* old. Carbon dating put it at around 450 BC, with the handwritten notes coming in later, obviously. Grandad and Van Burren split the find, with Grandad keeping the stone and Van Burren keeping the map. It was the only way they could think of to keep things above board in the partnership. Though Grandad said he always figured Van Burren got the better end of the deal, since the map could lead them to wherever Atlantis might be."

"And how does Atlantis figure into this, exactly? Where did they get the idea that the map leads to a mythical lost city?"

"Some of Edison's notes mention it," Gail said. "My grandfather and Van Burren were able to have some of the map's non-English writing translated. We've been calling that language 'Atlantean,' though the people we engaged to help us were skeptical. The notes on the map mention a great city, with 'treasures and wonders.' There's nothing on the map to say where that city was, exactly, and Edison's notations led them to a set of ruins that were unlikely to be the real thing. They found a few more artifacts that contained the same symbols as the stone, however. Most were junk. But one piece had a small bit of the Atlantean language that happened to appear with its translation in *Khmer*, the Cambodian language."

"A Rosetta Stone," Kotler mused, awed.

"Not a very good one, unfortunately," Gail said. "It didn't provide enough to fully translate the symbols on the stones, or the map. Just more hints. My grandfather used to joke that if Edison couldn't find Atlantis, what hope did two old soldiers have? Especially since they didn't even *trust* each other. Grandad kept journals and pieces hidden from Van Burren, and he was absolutely certain Van Burren did the same."

Kotler was thinking about everything he'd just learned, along with all of the implications. Finally he shook his head. "This is a lot of information to take in all at once, Gail. But to make sure I have it straight—your grandfather held on to the stone, which is half of a set. Van Burren held on to the map, which actually had all the hints, answers, and information the two of them needed. It sounds like

Van Burren was pretty smart. He knew where the real value was."

"But he won't let anyone see that map now," Gail said. "And he's demanding this stone."

"Which means ..." Kotler mused for a moment. "He's discovered something new from the map, and needs the stone to verify it ... or to access it." He thought again, then looked up at her. "What about the *other* stone? The one in the photograph?"

"It's in a private collection," Gail said. "Or it was. But the owner is anonymous, and I've had no luck in reaching him."

"Where was it found?" Kotler asked.

Gail let out a sigh. "Here," she said. "In New Jersey, actually."

"Wait," Kotler said. "You're telling me that an ancient artifact that could lead to the discovery of *Atlantis* was found in *New Jersey?*"

She laughed lightly. "Well, not just laying around on the Atlantic City Boardwalk or anything. It was part of Edison's 'dark estate.'"

Kotler sat back, amazed.

Edison's official estate was essentially a matter of public record. Everything the inventor had created, all of his business holdings, everything that was of any value when the man died was left to his living family—among them his son, Charlie. But there had long been rumors of a more *secretive* estate, and one that had been left to unnamed persons in Edison's life. Charlie, perhaps, was one of the recipients. But according to the lore, there were others.

The 'dark estate' was more urban legend than anything, by Kotler's estimate. But the rumors were that Edison had a cache of off-the-books projects that he deemed far too dangerous, or far too unready, for public consumption. Inventions that were ahead of the era by centuries, research that opened up dangerous lines of exploration into new fields of science, and journals that cataloged secrets Edison thought the world could not yet handle.

Kotler had actually spent a bit of time studying Edison, as well as Nikola Tesla, Henry Ford, Philo Farnsworth, and many other early inventors. They often had tragic lives, and dramatic personal histories. In the case of men like Edison and Tesla, they also tended to have bitter rivalries, as well as long and solid backgrounds in hidden and secretive research on a global and historic scale.

They were among some of the first Westerners to discover lost cultures and civilizations, and potentially lost ancient technologies and disciplines, in a continuous pursuit of new science and discovery.

They were *fascinating*.

And now, it seemed, Edison's penchant for exploration and research might just unravel one of the biggest riddles of history.

If what Gail was telling him was even remotely true, Thomas Edison might have known the truth about Atlantis.

And now a wealthy real estate mogul and antiquities smuggler wanted that truth all to himself.

CHAPTER 2

MANHATTAN, UPPER EAST SIDE

"You're sure you'll be alright?" Kotler asked.

He and Gail had shared an Uber back to the apartments, stopping half a block away, where they both exited. Kotler wasn't quite ready to face the press just yet, and so Gail would walk the rest of the way, sparing him the onslaught. Kotler would walk the other way, moving toward the hospital where Eloi Coelho was being treated.

Gail smiled. "Absolutely. Thank you for chatting with me."

"I want to do more than that," Kotler said. "I want to *help* you."

"I hoped you would, but I'm not sure how," Gail said. "I'm not even sure what it is I really want to come out of this. I … I mostly want to vindicate my grandfather, if I can. He always felt that he'd made a pact with the devil. Since he died, Van Burren has shown me exactly what kind of devil he really is. He's put a lot of pressure on me to get this stone."

Kotler nodded. "You should put that somewhere safe while this is going on," he said. "A man like Van Burren—he would have no trouble hiring someone to steal it from you."

Gail glanced around, as if just hearing the words might trigger someone stepping out, gun in hand, demanding the stone. "I hadn't really thought about that," she admitted. "I didn't want to leave it in the apartment, for that reason. But it didn't occur to me that it might not be safe to carry it around." She thought for a moment, biting her lip, then looked at Kotler. "Can you take it?"

Kotler's eyebrows arched in surprise. "I .. well, yes, I can. But I'm a little surprised you would ask. You barely know me."

She waved this off. "I'm a quick study, when it comes to people. And I've followed your career for quite a while now. Even before this Viking quest you've been on. I know you're a man with integrity, and that you have your own means. I actually tracked you down specifically to have you help me with this. So it's nothing to have you hold it in safe keeping."

Kotler thought about this for a moment. "I'm not sure it's actually all that safe with me either. If Van Burren happens to know that you're talking to me, then we're right back in the same boat. But I know someone I can trust, who has the resources to keep the stone safe. He might also be able to help in investigating who has the second half, and what Van Burren's intentions might be."

"Who is he?" Gail asked.

Kotler looked at her, and then shook his head. "I don't think I should say. He might not want to get involved. But if he does, it's best to have a firewall between you and him. Is it enough to say that I trust him with my life?"

Gail thought about this, then nodded. "If you trust him that much, then I trust him too."

"Good," Kotler said.

Gail handed him the stone, wrapped in a bit of tissue paper. To anyone watching, it might look for all the world as if she'd just handed him a small gift, maybe chocolates or some other sweet.

Kotler slipped it into his pocket quickly and casually. "I'll take it to him now. I have someone I need to see today, and my friend is on the way. We should exchange numbers. I can call you later and we can chat about what to do next."

She smiled. "Is this your way of asking me out?"

Kotler blushed. The last woman he'd felt any romantic compunctions toward had been Evelyn Horelica—and that had more or less come to a close even *before* she was kidnapped and held hostage by a mad billionaire. Evelyn had withdrawn after her rescue, and she and Kotler had not done much more than email each other since. The emails were short and unemotional. Kotler had first tried to fall back into the rhythms of their previous relationship, with flirting and innuendo taking reign. But Evelyn had refused to play along. She'd been too hurt, too damaged by the events surrounding the Coelho Medallion. And despite the fact that Kotler had been instrumental in her rescue, she couldn't bear to spend time with him. It was too fresh, and he was too much of a reminder of all that had happened.

There was no shortage of women who found Kotler appealing. But most were not the sort that Kotler preferred. They sought fame, as well as a lifestyle of excitement and adventure. Kotler didn't have the heart to explain just how *boring* his life was at the moment. He yearned to be back out in the field again, to explore ruins or to unearth some hidden treasure.

And, if he was honest, these women were not all that attractive to him. They were *beautiful*, that was certain. Most tended toward supermodel figures, and *Vogue* features. But they lacked the sort of *intellectual* beauty he preferred.

They couldn't keep up with him in conversation, or they had little to no interest in his work. And try as he might,

Kotler could never quite take interest in their pursuits either. He cared little about fashion, and less about celebrity gossip or A-list parties—the primary interests of most of the women who showed they were attracted to him.

His wealth and his recent fame drew these women out of every corner of Manhattan, and Kotler couldn't muster more than just pure physical attraction to them. And if that was all they could offer, he was less than interested.

Gail, on the other hand …

"You can't blame a man for trying," Kotler said, smiling.

Gail smiled back, and the two of them did exchange numbers. Kotler would be in touch. Definitely. Gail was just his type, after all. Beautiful, intelligent, and holding the key to potentially solving an age-old mystery.

Hubba-hubba.

Kotler stepped out of the elevator of the FBI's main New York offices, and strolled through a corridor of cubicles and office doors. He had checked in on the ground floor, going through security and metal detectors, and waiting for a guard to call up and make sure he was cleared for entry. So there was really no way for him to drop in on Agent Roland Denzel unannounced.

Denzel had been promoted since their adventure beneath Cheyenne Mountain, and had graduated to one of the actual offices. There had been a bit of remodeling since Kotler had been here last, and the offices had shifted somewhat from their drab 'cubicle nation' decor to a much more attractive and modern layout of glass and metal. Offices such as Denzel's were not much for privacy, unless one were to close the vertical blinds.

Denzel currently had the blinds open and pulled aside. He was sitting at his desk, working at a laptop, when Kotler knocked lightly on the glass door.

"Sit," Denzel said, without looking up.

Kotler smiled lightly, chuckling a bit as he shook his head, and sat.

It was almost always like this with Denzel. A sort of ongoing alpha-male head butting that inevitably trended toward frat-house level banter. Denzel knew that Kotler had no interest in proving who was the dominant man, however. In fact, Denzel himself didn't seem to really mind playing second fiddle, when the circumstances called for it. Neither man was given to ego of that sort—they had egos for other things entirely.

But they both played the game anyway, because it was fun, and it was the type of bond they shared. Kotler could tell from Denzel's body language that he was fighting to keep up the ruse, to keep focused on his computer, and to keep from turning and facing Kotler.

Eventually he broke composure and turned, refocusing his reserves of willpower to keep from smiling.

"You're happy to see me," Kotler said.

Now Denzel really did scowl. "You *always* think that," he replied. Then he smiled, and rose from his chair, extending a hand.

Kotler did the same, and after they shook, Denzel moved around the desk and shut the glass door, then took a seat across from Kotler, in one of the other chairs. "What's up? I haven't heard from you in almost a month."

"I got tied up with closing loops at the Coelho dig," Kotler said. "And the press have been on me every second since I've been home."

"Fame getting you down?" Denzel grinned.

"I never cared about fame," Kotler said, waving this off. "I just wanted to discover everything I could about that Viking city."

"Have you found something new?" Denzel asked.

Kotler shook his head. "Nothing all that important. The

discoveries are all being made by the on-site team now. I haven't been there in a long while. I've wrapped up my part in it and now I'm on to the next project."

"Already?" Denzel asked. "What is it this time? Roman soldiers in New York's sewers?"

"Everyone knows their invasion was pushed back by the alligator people," Kotler said, deadpan.

The banter was normal for the two of them, and it felt right. They hadn't known each other long, but they'd suffered through trauma and even injury together. They were bonded by combat. Friends, because how could they *not* be friends?

"So what's going on?" Denzel asked. "You have that 'I've got something important to explain' look."

"I met a woman today. Gail McCarthy. She's the grand-daughter of ..."

"Edward McCarthy," Denzel interrupted, suddenly losing some of his relaxed composure. "Partner to Richard Van Burren. The real estate czars."

"Right," Kotler said. "I take it they're on your radar?"

"Van Burren is," Denzel said. "McCarthy died before I could find any dirt on him."

This wasn't good. If Denzel was already predisposed to think of McCarthy as a villain, he might not be open to helping Gail.

"Well, this didn't start out the way I thought it would," Kotler said. "I was hoping to ask you a favor, but now I'm wondering if I should just leave quietly."

"Ask," Denzel said. "No promises."

Kotler studied him for a moment. His body language was tense, meaning that whatever his reasons for investigating McCarthy and Van Burren, it was something pretty awful. Kotler knew Denzel well enough to know how dedicated he was, and how honest. If Kotler showed him the stone, what would he do with it?

"I have something. It's a small piece to a bigger puzzle. I have no idea if it's in any way related to your case, but it *is* part of something I'm researching. I wanted to ask if you could protect it somehow. I would still want access to it, however. For study."

"What is it?" Denzel asked.

Kotler glanced around, and Denzel caught the hint. He stood and closed the blinds, protecting them from any prying eyes. Kotler took the stone out of his pocket then, unwrapping it and laying it on the desk between them.

"What is it?" Denzel asked again, reaching out and lifting the stone in its wrapper, examining it under the light of a small lamp before placing it back on the desk.

"Well, I can't say for sure just yet. But if Gail's story checks out, this could be a clue to finding …"

Kotler paused, not sure of what was going to come next. He wasn't even sure if he *believed* the story of Atlantis yet. It was intriguing, and this artifact was worth checking out. The whole story was worth exploring, actually. And Kotler really had no fear of what his peers or the rest of academia or the scientific community might think about his pursuits. They were going to disapprove regardless of what he uncovered, if he was being honest with himself.

But he found, oddly, that he cared an awful lot about what *Denzel* thought.

"What?" Denzel asked, impatient.

"Ok, look … I'm the messenger on this one, ok? So what I say next is just the information I have on hand, and not yet my firm opinion."

"Enough with the caveats and disclaimers, Kotler. What *is it?*"

"Atlantis," Kotler said.

Denzel looked at him, then to the stone, and then back to Kotler. He rolled his eyes. "Got it," he said. "If you just wanted to grab lunch or something you could have asked. I don't have time to screw around with gags."

Kotler was staring at him. "Not a gag," he said. The intensity of his voice was solid, steady. He continued to look at Denzel's face, and Denzel returned the look. Denzel wasn't quite as good as Kotler when it came to reading body language, but he knew how to tell when someone was lying, or when they were serious.

"Go on," Denzel said, cautious.

Kotler nodded, then told Denzel the whole story—everything he'd learned from Gail.

When he was done, the two of them sat back. Denzel had his fingers cupped over his mouth, thinking. Kotler watched, wondering what his friend thought of all of it.

"Coffee?" Denzel asked, shooting a glance at the closed blinds.

Kotler nodded.

Denzel stood and opened the door, then waved for Kotler to follow.

They went to a small break room, where Denzel produced two mugs with the FBI logo emblazoned on them. He filled these from a pot that Kotler suspected had been on low simmer for most of the morning. The coffee was practically rancid—burnt and thick to the point where it might better be described as motor oil.

"Dear God, Denzel," Kotler said, his face soured. "You think this is *coffee?*"

Denzel sipped his cup, winced, gave a slight nod, and then quietly poured his cup into the sink. "*Real* coffee?"

"I know a place nearby," Kotler said.

They sat in a booth in the back. Kotler marveled briefly over the fact that this was the second coffee shop he'd visited in just the past two hours. An occupational hazard, perhaps. He couldn't complain.

They both sat with cups of plain, black pour-over coffee, and Kotler watched Denzel take his first sip, closing his eyes and taking it in like ambrosia.

"Better," Denzel said. He looked at Kotler, and his expression changed slightly, becoming more intense. "I think we'd better talk," he said.

"I thought we were *already* talking," Kotler replied, smiling.

"But now we *really* need to talk. Because you've somehow become associated with an active case, and I'm bound by oath to investigate you and your relationship with Richard Van Burren."

Kotler considered this for a moment, then nodded. "Ok. Here it is. I've never met the man. Before meeting Gail McCarthy this morning, for the first time, I had only a magazine article's knowledge of who Van Burren actually *was*. I know he was a veteran. And I know he was one of the founders of a huge real estate business. And I know that he's been investigated for *years* for various smuggling operations, but always somehow exonerated. Beyond that, nothing. Unless you count what I learned today."

"And what did you learn today?" Denzel asked.

Kotler thought for a moment. If he shared what he and Gail had discussed, it could be incriminating for Gail. Kotler didn't know her well, but his instincts told him she was innocent in whatever crimes Van Burren had committed. And though his instincts were far from infallible, he trusted his gut on this one.

"Roland," Kotler said …

"Right now," Denzel said, "I'm Agent Denzel. Right now, we're not friends. At this moment, you're being investigated by the FBI."

Kotler considered this. "Well, it isn't the first time. Do

you suspect I'm part of Van Burren's operation?" Kotler asked.

Denzel shook his head. "No. But I have to get this part out of the way first."

Now Kotler understood. Denzel was taking a hard tack, because he needed his case to be above board, and water tight. He couldn't allow there to be any hint that he had turned away a potential lead, or covered anything up, simply because a friend was involved in the case.

"Agent Denzel," Kotler said, picking up the formality, "I would be happy to cooperate fully with the FBI regarding this investigation. I'll go on record with it. I'll share everything I know, which isn't much. But I'd like something in return."

Denzel's brow creased, curious. "And what is that?"

"Well, I'm going to turn over the stone to you for safe keeping. And I'll report anything I learn that's relevant to the case. But I'd like to be brought into the investigation."

Denzel laughed. "Absolutely not. You're not an agent, Kotler."

"No," Kotler said. "But I *am* an expert. And you're going to need one for this case."

"You have no idea what this case is," Denzel said, laughing. "You don't know why I'm investigating Van Burren."

"Can you tell me?" Kotler asked.

Denzel shook his head. "Not on your life."

"Ok," Kotler said. "What if I tell *you*? Will that be tantamount to me confessing to some kind of inside knowledge? Can I tell you as an informed expert? Will you treat me as an expert witness, rather than as a suspect?"

Denzel nodded. "You got it. I'll make you a consultant, if you want."

That was what Kotler wanted to hear. As a consultant, he

might not be privy to everything the FBI had on this case, but
he'd at least be able to stick around, conducting his *own* research,
without stepping on the FBI's toes and maybe landing in prison.

This entire conversation had been orchestrated to put
them right here, Kotler realized. Denzel had arranged this for
Kotler's protection, and to enlist Kotler's help, but it all had
to unfold in just the right way. Kotler admired Denzel's cleverness—he knew his friend was smart, but he'd never quite
thought of him as *crafty*.

"Ok," Kotler said. "Here's what I think. Van Burren has
been smuggling everything from drugs to weapons to works
of art into the country for decades, and lately there's been an
increase in blackmarket gold and antiquities. McCarthy was
a suspect in this as well, but his sudden death put an end to
that line of inquiry. And his death has a pallor of suspicion
attached to it—it might not have been natural causes after
all, so that has to be vetted. And finally, there's wind of something *big* happening—a huge payout in the works that has
the blackmarkets buzzing. Van Burren's name is whispered
every now and then, but no one is confirming anything.
They just know that he's on to something, and he's on the
hunt for something. He's close to cracking whatever it is that
stands between him and the largest score of his career. The
FBI have gotten wind of this, but they don't have enough to
pin anything on him, or bring him down. How am I doing?"

Denzel was staring at Kotler intently, but also glancing
from side to side, to ensure they weren't being heard.

Kotler had leaned in and kept his voice at a whisper, so
that only Denzel could hear. The effect, however, had been to
intensify the conversation and raise tension.

Kotler was making this up as he went, of course. *All* of it.
But he knew men like Van Burren—he'd dealt with smugglers of all types, in his career. He hated to admit it, but
sometimes he *used* smugglers like Van Burren, to help move

materials out of one country and into another. Usually these were goods that had been stolen in the first place, and Kotler was arranging for them to be moved back to where they belonged. But the network needed for this kind of work, the process involved in moving treasures from place to place—it was all the same, whether done for good or for evil. Men like Van Burren were a necessary part of Kotler's work at times.

"How the hell do you *do* that?" Denzel asked.

"It's a hobby."

Denzel shook his head, looking around. "Ok, not bad. And no, I don't think you're involved in any way. But to be honest, I actually *could* use someone who is an expert in this stuff. The things he's bringing in—there's no record of any of it. The buyers are typically collectors, and we've put some phony buyers in a couple of times. But they come back with stuff that we can't actually use in a bust. No one is reporting anything stolen, and nothing is recognizable as being part of a culture heist."

"So he has a source that isn't culturally recognized," Kotler said.

"Right," Denzel replied.

"Like the piece I brought you," Kotler said.

Denzel nodded.

"Van Burren is after that piece," Kotler said.

That got Denzel's interest. "Is he now? Well, that raises all sorts of interesting possibilities."

"I told Gail I was giving it to a friend to keep safe. So here's what I'd ask—please don't get it blown up or stolen."

"That does take a lot of the fun out of it," Denzel shook his head.

"And I will happily help you bust Van Burren, if you will allow me to pursue any leads we find that can lead us to Atlantis."

Denzel scoffed. "You really believe in that?"

Kotler shrugged. "Call it a code name, if you like. We don't know what Van Burren has found, but we know he needs that stone to find more of it. 'Operation Atlantis' is as good a name as any, isn't it?"

"Its a terrible name and you know it," Denzel said. "That name will never appear on any official FBI file folder."

"But you'll bring me into the fold?"

Denzel nodded. "I will. I'll get the papers lined up so you can officially be an FBI consultant. You'll even make a small salary."

Kotler waved this off. "I don't need money, just access."

Denzel shrugged. "It's required. Give it to charity, if it makes you feel better."

Kotler nodded. "I like that." He grinned at Denzel. "And I like working with you in an 'official capacity' for once. Especially one where I'm not being investigated as a potential terrorist."

Denzel chuckled and said, "Just don't do anything stupid, like get kidnapped and tortured."

"I'll do my best. So I should tell you, then, that there's another stone, nearly identical. A second half."

"Who has it?" Denzel asked.

"That was one of the things I was hoping you could help with. Gail thinks it was part of Edison's estate."

"Edison … *Thomas Alva* Edison?"

"Why does everyone throw in 'Alva' as if there were so many other Thomas Edison's in history?" Kotler asked.

"Same guy?"

"Same guy," Kotler agreed. "Van Burren has a map that was once owned by Edison, and even has Edison's hand-written notes on it. I think that's how he's found whatever it is he's found. And I think he's discovered something that requires both of those stones to unlock."

"And you have one of them," Denzel said.

"It doesn't belong to me, but yes. And technically, *you* have it now. What we're missing is the other stone. And the map."

"I may not be able to do much about the map. Unless someone reports it stolen, it's Van Burren's private property. But the other stone ... maybe I can help with that."

"Good," Kotler said. "I'll have Gail send the photo."

Denzel nodded, sipping his coffee again. "Good," he said. "Let's get to work."

CHAPTER 3

KOTLER HAD BEGGED OFF FROM DENZEL SO THAT HE could keep the one appointment he'd actually had on his calendar for the day. With all the side-tracking, between Gail and Denzel, not to mention avoiding the press, Kotler found himself arriving quite a bit later than he had intended.

New York-Presbyterian Hospital was a learning hospital, with ties to some of the most prestigious Ivy League schools in the region. A fact that, Kotler was certain, was a prominent consideration for the care of Dr. Eloi Coelho. The man loved academia, loved all forms of learning, and had been a headliner for numerous high profile university events. With his name still commanding quite a bit of press after the Viking affair in Colorado, there had been relatively few barriers to entry for him anywhere. Coming here had been his own choice.

Kotler nodded to the nurse as he entered Coelho's room. She gave him a stern look—an expression that Kotler could have translated even without his training in reading body language. *Don't get him worked up. Don't give him any stress. Don't stay too long.*

Kotler was perfectly willing to obey all three unspoken directives.

"Dr. Coelho," Kotler said quietly, sliding a chair close to the old man's bed.

Coelho opened his eyes, and rolled them toward Kotler. "Dan," he said, his voice quiet and hoarse, and tinged with the Portuguese accent that made him sound somehow wise and gentle with every word. "I had not expected you to come. What a wonderful surprise."

Kotler nodded, and reached to pat the aged hand of his friend.

Coelho had been in and out of hospitals for months now, from one complication after another following a gunshot—his injury sustained while he and Kotler were evading capture.

Kotler felt a pang of guilt over his friend's injuries and condition, considering he was there when Coelho took the bullet. Everyone assured Kotler that Coelho would have died if not for him being there, but Kotler wasn't so sure. The men who had shot him were there to capture Coelho, and Kotler had been the one to convince Coelho to run. Running was what had gotten him shot.

Kotler was convinced that ultimately they did the right thing. But now, seeing Coelho lying in this bed, tubes connecting him to various machines and IV bags—Kotler wasn't so sure of his choices.

They chatted for some time. Kotler caught Coelho up on the goings-on of the dig. Coelho was grateful for the information. "They took my iPad," he said, irritated. "They won't let me watch the television or read the paper. I'm stuck here with no data."

"I know that has to be difficult, but you need the rest."

Coelho waved a hand at this. He looked so *frail* at the moment. So *old*. Before being shot, he had looked fairly fit and robust, considering his age. But months of dealing with health issues had weathered him, worn him away like rubbing sandstone.

Kotler didn't want to stay too long. He knew that Coelho would need rest. So he kept the conversation short, and when Coelho's eyes drooped a bit, Kotler stood and said his goodbyes. He called the nurse back in, and then he left the room.

It had been a pleasant conversation with an old friend. And, Kotler suspected, it might be the last. Coelho's story was drawing to a close, Kotler feared. His friend might not be around much longer.

This made Kotler very sad, of course, but it also made him *angry*. The events surrounding his encounter with Anwar Adham, in the foothills of Colorado, still felt fresh in his mind, despite having happened nearly a year ago. Adham had kidnapped and tortured Kotler, demanding he provide translations and information. And it was Adham's men who had shot Coelho. Kotler was having a hard time forgetting all of that. So his sadness about his friend was tinged with anger that had no focus. Adham had died in that underground river, by Kotler's own hand. Justice, Kotler knew.

And yet justice hadn't settled the feeling that wrapped itself around Kotler's heart. There was still that burning ember that threatened to ignite him at any moment. It singed the edges of his patience and tolerance, making it difficult for Kotler to let small slights pass.

This was becoming evident primarily in his dealings with the academic world.

Since the events in Pueblo had come to a head, and Kotler had spearheaded the endeavor to uncover and explore more of the underground Viking city there, his relationship with academic and scientific colleagues had become more and more strained. There was resentment from the community, that he—an upstart, self-employed, self-empowered independent researcher—was gaining so much notoriety from his findings. Kotler was touching the public in a way that his colleagues had never been able to accomplish, and many resented it.

He found that many of his papers were being rejected in peer review. His invitations to academic and fundraising events were suddenly lost before they were sent. His contacts within certain universities were becoming difficult to reach.

The academic community was famous for blacklisting individuals who did not conform to the status quo, but Kotler had always been able to stay outside of that. He'd always had good relationships with notable individuals within the community, and that had made it possible for him to bypass the usual cliques and get things through. But the story surrounding the Coelho Medallion had been too sensational, and had contradicted the findings and research of too many researchers and historians. It had put too much pressure on too many people, making life uncomfortable.

The result was a boycott.

Kotler had always marveled at the fact that despite all data and facts, some groups would insist on delusion rather than accept change. He had always held out higher hopes for academia and science. But in the end, scientists were also human—and humans could be biased and prideful, just like anyone else.

Kotler stepped from the elevator and out into the hospital's lobby, making his way past reception to the glass doors that led to the street. Once outside, he took out his phone, intending to hire an Uber. He wanted to get back home and get some rest before jumping into the research regarding the Edison map and the stones. Denzel had promised to email Kotler with anything he could find about the owner of the second stone, and had been grateful for the leads provided by Gail and her private investigator.

Gail had been grateful, too, and had told Kotler that Van Burren had tried calling her several times, and that Ernest—their doorman—had reported that two men representing Van Burren had stopped by to ask about her, while Kotler and Gail had been having coffee.

Van Burren's intense interest in the stone was evident. What wasn't so clear was how far he was willing to go to get it.

Kotler planned to have a late night. At the moment, all he wanted was to return to his apartment, take a short nap, and then start parsing the information he had, along with anything Denzel might have sent him.

Before he could finish calling for a car, however, a large, black sedan pulled to the curb, and a man stepped up from behind him.

"Get in," the man said.

Kotler felt the man's large hand grip his arm, a vice that Kotler instinctively knew could tighten further. The message was clear—this was not a request.

"Getting in," Kotler said, and the man stepped around just enough to open the car door for him. Kotler ducked his head a bit, and dropped into the back seat next to a man who appeared to be in his mid- to late-seventies. Kotler had seen enough photos and video of the man to recognize him immediately.

"Richard Van Burren," Kotler said.

"Dr. Kotler!" Van Burren said, his voice tinged with a North Carolina accent. "Well, it's really something to meet you, son. I've been following your work down in Colorado. Vikings?" Van Burren chuckled and shook his head. "That's some fascinating stuff, brother."

Kotler nodded, and glanced to the side as the man from

the street shut the car door and then climbed into the passenger seat up front. The car pulled away from the curb, the driver easing into traffic and then speeding away in the first gap he could find.

"What can I do for you, Mr. Van Burren?" Kotler asked.

Van Burren chuckled. "Well, I can't say I don't appreciate getting right to the point, son. I think you have something that belongs to me. I'm here to ask you—*politely*, of course— to give it back."

"I'm afraid I don't know what you're talking about, Mr. Van Burren," Kotler said. "As far as I'm aware, this is the first time we've ever met."

Van Burren nodded. "That's true. But I believe you met the granddaughter of my former partner? Abigail McCarthy?"

"I believe she prefers 'Gail.' Yes, we had coffee today."

Van Burren made a regretful sound, shaking his head. "Oh, I *miss* coffee. The doctors won't let me have a drop of it these days, though. Ulcers. You understand."

"I really don't, Mr. Van Burren," Kotler said. "But here's what I *do* understand. You just abducted me. And that tells me something very important. We're not friends. So why don't you stop talking to me as if we were?"

There was a brief pause, and then Van Burren chuckled again. To Kotler it sounded a bit like a dog growling over his bowl. Happy to be fed, wary of strangers.

"Fair enough," Van Burren said. "Alright, Dr. Kotler. We'll dispense with the pleasantries. Now, where is the stone?"

"I don't have it," Kotler said. "I've put it in a safe place."

"And what safe place would that be, Dr. Kotler?" Van Burren asked.

"The FBI has it," Kotler said.

He watched Van Burren as he said this, and without

doubt the man tensed. Kotler saw the minute muscles of his face tighten, his jaw clench. And he noticed that Van Burren's right hand, which had been draped loosely in his lap, clenched quickly, as if he were struggling to keep from forming a fist.

Aggressive behavior. Van Burren wasn't used to anyone being impertinent or defiant.

"Well now, why would you go and give it the *FBI*? It's just an old *heirloom*," Van Burren said with a drawl. "Something Edward and I used to trade back and forth, as far back as our Army days. I just wanted to have something to remember my friend by. There's nothing untoward about it."

"No, I agree," Kotler said. "When Gail gave it to me for safekeeping, I felt nothing untoward about it at all."

"It wasn't hers to *give*," Van Burren said, his voice stern. Kotler imagined this was how Van Burren talked to people who worked for him, and people whom he negotiated with. It was a fallback for Van Burren—his most used card.

"I don't know what sort of arrangement you had with Edward McCarthy," Kotler said. "But that stone was in his possession when he died, and he left it to his granddaughter. Whatever its origin, at the moment it belongs to her. And she's put it in my care. Unless you can provide some sort of legal documentation that demonstrates your ownership of it, I'm going to make sure it stays safe with the FBI."

Van Burren studied him for a moment, his face a tangle of suppressed anger and frustration. Then suddenly that tension broke, and he smiled lightly and shook his head. "You kids," he said. "You play a little in the sandbox and you think you know the desert." He leaned toward Kotler, his eyes blazing and intense. "You don't want to screw with me, Kotler. You have no idea what I'm capable of."

Kotler took this in, then shook his head. "Van Burren, I don't *care* what you think you're capable of. You don't frighten me. I've known *actual* scary people, and do you know what all of them had in common? Not one of them had to *tell me* how scary they were."

The car had stopped for a light, and Kotler looked out of the window. He opened the door and stepped out before Van Burren could say anything. The bodyguard up front attempted to open his door and Kotler kicked this closed before the man had a chance to exit.

Kotler leaned back into the vehicle, and Van Burren waved to the bodyguard, indicating everything was alright.

Kotler said, "I know what you've been up to, Van Burren. I know what you've found. And I know why you need the stone. I will personally make sure that you never get your hands on it."

Van Burren stared hard, trying to burn through Kotler. Then he smiled, and shook his head. "I'm sure you'll do your best," he said. "That's what men like you do. Your *best.*" He chuckled. "But I've already found what I'm looking for, Dr. Kotler. All you're doing is slowing down access."

Kotler straightened and closed the car door, then walked away.

He was a few blocks from the hospital now, and his apartment was several blocks on the other side. He could either take the subway, or call a car. For now, he slipped into a café, and ordered a glass of ice water and a cheese plate.

He'd had enough coffee today. He'd had enough of a lot of things.

Kotler was biding time, waiting until Van Burren's car was far away, but also waiting until his own nerves settled.

He hadn't been lying. Van Burren didn't scare him. Kotler had met men like him many times before, and he knew they were capable of violence, even if by remote control. But Kotler had seen a lot of violence, had been the victim of much of it. He had been in the presence of truly frightening men, and suffered at their hands, and had survived. He would survive Van Burren as well.

What had his adrenaline up at the moment, however, was what he had *learned* from Van Burren.

The man said he had *found what he was looking for*. And, if Gail was right, that meant he'd found *Atlantis*.

Kotler brought out his smartphone and started tapping an email to Denzel.

Roland,

Just had an impromptu meeting with Van Burren. He picked me up outside of New York-Presbyterian Hospital. But the important part is that he just confirmed he's found what he's looking for. He needs the stones for access.

We should look at his travel records for the past six months. Can we do that?

Also, Gail may need protection. I have a bad feeling.

Kotler

He sent the email, and then sipped his water and savored a pungent cheese. In a moment there was a ping from his phone.

It was a response from Denzel.

Sounds like you'll need protection, too.

Stay put. I have agents nearby who can drive you home

Kotler sipped his water again, and tried not to wonder at the fact that Denzel already had agents nearby, despite Kotler never having said where he was, exactly. He knew his FBI friend thought ahead, and he knew that Denzel also had Kotler's best interest at heart. He could be forgiven for being a little over protective.

Kotler spent the next few minutes creating a new folder in Evernote, gathering what he knew so far in notes, photos, and speculations. It wasn't much. Not yet. But he had a feeling this folder was going to get a lot bigger, fast.

Another chime from his phone, and it was again a message from Denzel.

Scratch that. The car is taking you to the airport. We found the other stone.

Kotler smiled. He hadn't fully realized it, but in the months since he'd been working at the Coelho dig site, he had started to feel a bit pent up. Most of his career, he'd had the latitude to roam wherever he liked, to explore whatever avenues interested him. Lately, he'd been more or less locked into one project, on a leash of his own devising.

But now he was about to step into another adventure, and it felt *thrilling.* It was waking up that part of him that loved to explore, to dare against the darkness of the world, and to seek out light in the deepest caverns of history.

He wondered briefly what that meant about him— whether it defined him as some sort of adrenaline junky. But then his FBI escort arrived, and he found himself being driven to the airport. For the second time since knowing Roland Denzel, Kotler was about to travel at the FBI's behest, without so much as an overnight bag packed.

He really had to start carrying a bag with him at all times.

CHAPTER 4

HABBERSHAM ABBEY, VERMONT

KOTLER AND DENZEL WERE USHERED INTO A STUDY ON the ground floor of one of the largest estates Kotler had ever seen in the United States. It was an import—or so Kotler's impromptu research informed him. Every stone of the building had been carted over from Great Britain by a cargo ship in 1942, at the behest of a wealthy oil tycoon. It was a sprawling historic building with classic British architectural notes, and the standard upstairs/downstairs layout. Kotler had expected it to seem out of place in Vermont, but it connected perfectly with the landscape, as if Kotler and Denzel had somehow been transported to the English countryside.

The original owner, Frederick Habbersham, had been 'new money' at the time he'd purchased the Abbey and had it relocated. He was oil money—the filthiest kind, according to many of the historians who specialized in the period. But he was also an Anglophile, and had a driving passion for British history and culture—perhaps seeking out a connection with it to legitimize his fortune and new social status.

His contemporaries at the time thought he was insane,

and eventually they may have been proven out. Habbersham ended up losing his fortune, through a combination of bad investments, unfortunate scams, and—as if the rest weren't bad enough—he had fallen into massive gambling debts.

Habbersham eventually sold the estate to cover his losses, and it continued to be passed from owner to owner over the years, falling into disrepair, until finally it was purchased by Dr. Lester Rodham.

Rodham was a surgeon and inventor—creating a raft of medical devices by the time he was in his 50s, and living from the wealth generated by his patents. Like Habbersham, Rodham was an Anglophile. Unlike Habbersham, Rodham felt no compunction or need to legitimize his wealth. He was the sort of 'new money' that gained a great deal of respect and influence all on its own.

Purchasing and renovating Habbersham Abbey had been something Rodham felt he *deserved*, rather than something he felt he *needed*. That much was clear from the subdued decorative touches from space to space—austere rather than ostentatious. Despite the austerity—or perhaps because of it —the decor was all very elegant, making a statement. Rodham was an important man with good taste, and his home demonstrated that to intimidating effect.

"It looks like Downton Abbey," Denzel said.

Kotler looked at him, surprised. "*You* watched Downtown Abbey?"

Denzel's expression soured. "You think I don't have anything in my life that isn't the FBI or pain in the ass archeologists?"

Kotler chuckled.

The two of them were asked to wait in a large sitting room that was adorned with artwork and portraits, each period correct. Kotler was admiring a portrait of Habbersham himself—a thin, almost gaunt man who looked in no

way as if he could be connected to the Texas oil trade of the
1940s. He looked severe, and his eyes did have that glint of
intelligence to them. But from what Kotler had read on the
flight in, the man had lacked the proper business sense he
needed to keep his wealth and empire afloat. Kotler
suspected it was the classic story of sudden and new wealth
coming to someone who was used to struggle, and unused to
disposable income.

"Bets on how long he'll make us wait here?" Denzel
asked.

"Twenty minutes," Kotler quickly responded.

Denzel looked at him. "You seem pretty sure of that,"
he said.

"That's the average length of time someone with a superi-
ority complex will wait to prove they're in charge, in the presence of an actual authority figure."

"Meaning me?" Denzel asked.

"Your badge got us access where most people would be
turned away," Kotler said. "This space? It's designed to
impress visiting officials. Dr. Rodham likes to keep himself
distant from 'common folk.'"

"Ok, how could you possibly know that just from
looking around at a few paintings?" Denzel asked.

Kotler laughed. "Google," he said. "I researched this
place and Dr. Rodham on the way in. He has a few ... *detrac-
tors* online."

Denzel shrugged. "Doesn't everybody?"

Kotler smiled. He couldn't argue with that, though he
doubted many people had as many enemies as Dr. Rodham.
The man had managed to alienate a number of groups across
a wide playing field, from historians to soccer moms. In fact,
the only people he hadn't seemed to have made an enemy of
were lobbyists and the politicians they owned. There were
whispers of Dr. Rodham making a run for Governor of

Vermont soon, and from there a play for President of the United States.

Kotler thought these rumors might be just that, though, judging from Rodham's home. The man admired opulence, even if it was somewhat subdued. His power came from his personal image, not from his political standing. But perception is everything, and the perception that he was a powerful man who might someday sit in the highest office on the planet ... well, Kotler suspected that was the kind of image that Dr. Rodham wouldn't mind perpetuating.

Kotler sat patiently on one of the divans, which was placed against a wall opposite a large, leaded window. The window was a Tudor-style frame, Kotler noted. Not entirely native to the Abbey's design, but neither was it unexpected. It was likely an add-on from Habbersham's run of the place.

Denzel was not quite as patient. He paced, stopping to admire the odd scenic painting here and there, or to thumb through an accessible volume from among the book shelves lining one wall. Kotler watched him as he carefully and painstakingly opened each book, treating it with reverence.

Kotler hadn't know Denzel all that long, in the grand scheme of things, so there was still a great deal to learn about his friend. But he did genuinely like the man, and they had a sort of brother-in-arms bond after their ordeal in Colorado.

The most intriguing thing about Denzel, in Kotler's eyes, was that the man was so much more than he *appeared* to be. Kotler wasn't used to underestimating people, and it would be hazardous for anyone to underestimate Agent Roland Denzel. Despite knowing this, however, Kotler was continuously surprised by Denzel's range. He was a good friend to have, for sure. He'd make a terrible enemy, for certain. Kotler was glad he was the former, and far from the latter.

"Gentlemen," a deep and resonant male voice said from the far doorway.

Kotler looked up to see the butler, who was dressed in the standard livery of a servant from the period appropriate to Habbersham Abbey.

"Doctor Rodham will see you in the garden," the butler said, turning to lead them away from the sitting room.

Kotler glanced at Denzel, who once again had a soured expression on his face. As the two of them walked behind the butler, Denzel whispered, "Why have us wait in here if he was going to meet us in the garden?"

"Setting is very important," Kotler said. "He had to give us time to see how rich he is, and how much he values history. The garden is his way of showing he owns even the very nature here. And having us wait in the study and then emerge into natural light …"

"I get it, I get it," Denzel said, shaking his head. "Power play." He checked his watch. "It was twenty-*two* minutes, by the way."

Kotler smiled. "Well, I guess I'm getting rusty."

They were ushered outside to a large, natural-stone patio that had steps leading down into a vast and well-tended garden. Flowers of every description grew from large and ornate pots, surrounding a bricked circle providing a foundation for a table and several chairs. A man in his mid- to late-sixties sat in one of the chairs, facing the rest of the gardens—a huge and sprawling hedge maze dotted with blooming plants of every description. Beyond it all were the mountains and valleys of Vermont. It was stunning, Kotler had to admit—like looking at a Thomas Kinkade painting come to life.

The butler led the two of them to the table, offered them their seats, and then brought each of them a small porcelain saucer and cup, which he then filled with coffee. Kotler was starting to see a theme to his interactions with other humans these days—coffee was always on the menu.

"Gentlemen," Dr. Rodham said as he took a sip of his own coffee. "How may I help you?"

"As I explained to one of your people on the phone," Denzel said, "I'm Agent Roland Denzel, and this is Dr. Daniel Kotler. He's an FBI consultant, assisting me in an investigation. We believe that you may have an artifact that could also be useful in that investigation."

"And what, pray, would this artifact be?" Rodham responded. "I have many 'artifacts' here."

Denzel took out his phone and brought up the insurance photo that Gail McCarthy had provided. He slid the phone to Rodham, who took it in hand, using the tips of his fingers, as if he did not care to touch common things.

He took out a pair of reading glasses from his breast pocket, and perched them on the tip of his nose, looking down at the phone with an expression that read a great deal like distaste.

Kotler was amused by all of this. The man was putting on a show for the two of them, going out of his way to express disdain and a casual lack of concern or worry. It was more power play, of course, but it was so hammy, and so over the top, that Kotler wondered briefly if it were a prank. Dr. Rodham had certainly built his own small kingdom, and had certainly achieved a high level of success, but he still, some-how, acted as if he felt inadequate. He had to prove to every new soul that he was every bit as successful and powerful as he seemed to be. And he was overdoing it.

"Yes," Rodham said. "The Edison stone. I purchased this at an auction several years ago." He slid the phone back to Denzel, and folded the glasses to put back in his pocket. "I greatly admire Edison, and all of the American inventors," Rodham said. "They're a remarkable part of the American story, don't you agree?"

"Oh yes," Kotler said, speaking for the first time.

It had the effect of shifting Rodham's gaze, and his expression was that of someone discovering a fly on his plate, as if unsure of what it may have touched, or whether it even mattered.

Kotler smiled. He was reading Rodham's body language, deciphering a few things that Rodham was trying very hard to keep in check.

Seeing the 'Edison stone' had shaken him. Kotler saw it instantly. The *why* of it was something Kotler would have to suss out by different means, but he knew for certain that Rodham was not only hiding something, he was preparing to lie about it.

"Dr. Kotler," Rodham said, suddenly changing tack. "I have read a great deal about you lately."

"My books, perhaps?" Kotler asked, playing the game. "I always enjoy meeting my readers."

"*Press*," Rodham said in a disdainful tone, though whether that disdain was aimed at the press in general, or aimed at Kotler for being *mentioned* by the press, Kotler couldn't say. "You were involved in that Viking affair, in Colorado I believe?"

"Yes," Kotler said. He noted that Rodham had subtly shifted the conversation, so that he was controlling content. He had also belittled the 'Viking affair,' simultaneously showing his knowledge and his disdain of it.

Immediately Kotler adjusted his assessment of the man. He might be a bit self-aggrandizing, but he was also *sharp*. And he was *good*. In only a sentence or two, through tone and body language alone, he has managed to elevate himself while lowering Kotler to the level of someone common and inconsequential.

"It was quite a discovery," Kotler said. "What did you think of it?"

Rodham sniffed. "*Vikings*," he said, as if that were enough answer for anyone.

Kotler smiled and chuckled a bit. "They do get around," he said lightly, watching Rodham shift his attention back to Denzel.

"Dr. Rodham," Denzel said, seeming a little perplexed by the subtext of the conversation between Rodham and Kotler. "Would it be possible for us to examine the artifact? The Edison stone?"

Rodham sipped his coffee, then placed the cup on a saucer on the table. "I'm afraid that won't be possible," Rodham said.

"Is it no longer in your possession?" Denzel asked.

"Oh, I have it here on the estate," Rodham replied.

Denzel waited.

There was an uncomfortable beat, and Kotler half wanted to applaud. Denzel was fully capable of playing his *own* power games, and he was using one of his best tricks right now. Of the three of them, Denzel really *was* an authority figure here, with the badge to prove it. And though that badge was tucked safely away in the inside pocket of his suit coat, it still hung over Rodham as if it was the sword of Damocles.

Of course, ultimately even Denzel's authority as a Federal Agent was something of a bluff. They had quite a bit of latitude to pursue leads in this case, but without a warrant they couldn't force Rodham to turn anything over. The threat of that warrant was there, but it was like the threat of a gun still in its holster.

Kotler thought he had Rodham figured out, though. The man would resist any authority that wasn't backed up by something official. He would try to prove himself superior.

To get the man to turn over the Edison stone would require appealing to him *as* a superior.

"I'm afraid I don't see sufficient cause to risk damaging such a precious historic artifact," Rodham said, closing the trap that Kotler suspected he would use.

From the corner of his eye Kotler saw Denzel tense, but before his friend could say anything, Kotler spoke up.

"Mr. Rodham, we could get a warrant. It would only take a couple of hours. But I don't see why we should have to do that." Kotler could sense Denzel looking at him, questioning. "That stone could help us break this case, it's true. But aren't you also curious about its *origins?* Were you aware that there is *another* stone?"

"I was aware," Rodham said, and Kotler noted the slight uptick of interest in the man, though he kept it under control. "Do you … is it in your possession?"

Denzel spoke up, catching on to Kotler's tactic. "We're holding it as part of the investigation. But we would be willing to … well, let's say we could do an exchange of sorts. If you'll let us examine your stone, we'll let you examine ours."

Rodham considered this, then stared off into the gardens. "I would like to see it," he said quietly, and Kotler got the sense that he wasn't entirely speaking of the stones. Did he know what they could unlock? Was Rodham aware of the possibility of discovering *Atlantis?*

Rodham looked back at the two of them. "Bring your stone here, and I'll let you have access to mine."

"Ours is back in Manhattan …" Denzel started.

"That is the deal, Agent," Rodham said. "Now, if you'll excuse me, I have other matters to deal with. You'll be shown out."

The butler arrived then, as if he had been hovering just out of sight, waiting for his cue. "This way, sirs," he said, and led them back through the house and out to their vehicle.

Denzel slammed his door as Kotler settled into his seat.

"Great. If I'd known, I would have brought it *with us*. It would be faster to get the warrant."

"But less efficient," Kotler said.

Denzel stared at him, his expression tense.

"Rodham knows something about those stones. He will be more likely to share the information with us if we play nice."

Denzel scoffed and shook his head, starting the car. "Play nice," he said. "Right."

"We can get someone at the Bureau to courier the stone to us, can't we?" Kotler asked.

"It won't be until tomorrow," Denzel said.

Kotler nodded. They would wait. But the end result would be better than coming in with a show of force, he knew.

It was that far away look in Rodham's eyes that told Kotler there was something more here. Kotler wanted to learn what the man knew. That was worth waiting a day.

CHAPTER 5

BURLINGTON, VERMONT

THE BURLINGTON HARBOR HOTEL WASN'T THE MOST luxurious place Kotler had ever stayed, but it was far from the rat trap that Denzel had originally booked for them. Kotler had paid out of pocket to book a better hotel, and to upgrade them to a couple of suites.

"Call it a gift," Kotler said to Denzel when the two of them had checked in.

"I'm not allowed to accept gifts from consultants," Denzel said.

"A perk, then. Or a necessity. Your consultant needed to be in a better hotel, and you needed access to your consultant. Luckily there was this free room available."

"I'm sure there's a regulation against this somewhere, but I won't tell if you don't."

Kotler smiled. They made their way to the hotel bar, and as Denzel was off duty they both ordered drinks. They were sipping a top-shelf Scotch of the bartender's choosing, and Kotler was enjoying the downtime, without the risk of press or, hopefully, unscrupulous smugglers and real estate moguls dropping in.

"What did you think of Dr. Rodham?" Kotler asked.

Denzel made a face. "Arrogant. Entitled. And hiding something."

Kotler chuckled. "Can't argue with any of that. But what do you suppose he's hiding? He admitted to having the Edison Stone. That was essentially what we were after."

"The fact that he wouldn't show it to us means he's hiding something," Denzel said with conviction. "The fact that he changed his tune once he learned we had the other stone means that it's something connected to …"

He paused, his mouth open but his brain refusing to form the words.

Kotler waited. "Go ahead," he smiled.

Denzel scoffed, and shook his head. "Let's just say it's connected to whatever Van Burren is after."

Kotler laughed. "Come on, Roland. You can't even *say it?*"

"We have no proof that this has anything at all to do with Atlantis," Denzel said. "I'd be willing to compromise and say 'lost city.' Does that count?"

Kotler nodded. "Fair enough. It was Gail McCarthy who brought up Atlantis in the first place. It's possible she could be mistaken. But half the fun of this is the idea that Atlantis could be real, and that these artifacts could lead us there. Where's your sense of adventure?"

"I left it in a river under Cheyenne Mountain," Denzel said.

Kotler nodded and raised his glass. "To Eloi Coelho," Kotler said.

Denzel nodded and clinked his glass with Kotler's. "How's he doing?"

Kotler sipped his scotch and shook his head. "Not well. I expect he won't be with us much longer. I'm glad I had a chance to visit with him."

Denzel nodded, then cautiously asked, "And Evelyn?"

Kotler didn't look over at his friend, but instead stared into the amber liquid in his glass. His mouth quirked into a slight smile, and he shook his head. "She's had enough, I believe. More than."

Denzel was silent for a few seconds, then said, "It's a hard life, Kotler."

Kotler looked up to see his FBI friend staring at him with a hard expression.

Their relationship was still somewhat new, but they had spent enough time together, and gone through enough together, that Kotler felt he knew the man. He considered Denzel a friend. And he could read in the man's expression a sort of warning.

"You were Special Forces," Kotler said. "Before you were FBI."

Denzel nodded. "Six years. And you … I did some digging. You never served in the military."

Kotler chuckled brightly. "No. That was never the place for me."

"But you had training. Weapons training, tactics, survival and combat."

"Part of my upbringing, we'll say," Kotler replied.

"Why?" Denzel asked.

Kotler shrugged. "Have you ever been curious about something? Not your work, not your career, but something outside of the norm for you? Something you found fascinating enough to study in-depth?"

"You studied military tactics and weapons because you were, what, curious?"

Kotler shook his head, and laughed a bit. "Not just military tactics and weapons. Everything. I studied *everything*. I started following a bread crumb trail when I was a child, and it led to … well, it led me on a circuitous route through life."

"I'll say. Archeology, symbology, cryptography, quantum physics and quantum mechanics—not to mention military strategy, survival techniques, military-grade weapons, and a string of other things I don't fully understand. You studied criminal profiling and body language with some of the top professionals in the field—even some of the instructors at Quantico. In fact, from what I've seen, there aren't many subjects you *haven't* studied, and all of them were with the top professionals in those fields. So who were you trying to be when you grew up? Batman?"

Kotler laughed, this time loud enough that a couple of other patrons turned to see about the noise. Kotler chuckled a little as he leaned in, quieting the conversation. "I'd *love* to be Batman. But no, I'm telling you the whole truth. I have a tendency to become insatiably curious about things, and so I study them. I master them. It's something my father and mother used to encourage."

"And they were pretty eclectic themselves, from what I've seen," Denzel said.

Kotler shook his head. "Roland, I'm going to try not to take it personally that you saw fit to dig so deeply into my personal history."

Denzel shrugged. "Standard practice when vetting a CI. If you're going to be a consultant with the FBI, I need to know everything there is to know about you."

Kotler laughed again, nodding. "Fair enough. I've learned a bit about you as well."

Denzel's eyebrows shot up. "Oh? Did some digging?"

"A bit," Kotler said. "But most of what I need to know comes from interacting with you. I know you're an honorable man, if not always a trusting one. I know that you are ambitious, but also patient. I know that you took your role at the FBI because you wanted to do some real good, on a grander scale, and you didn't believe you could have as much impact on the front lines—either in combat or working with the DEA. You like to get out in the field, and get your hands dirty. But you want that work to have a greater reach than taking down the occasional drug lord, only to have someone else step right in to fill his shoes."

Denzel nodded. "Ok. I can live with all of that. But let's turn the lens back on Dr. Kotler for a moment. You're actually ok with Evelyn moving on without you."

Kotler came to a full stop, stiffening. It was rare that he didn't know what to say next, but this time Denzel had actually stumped him.

"You know that you're dangerous," Denzel said. "Don't you? You know that Evelyn was endangered *because* of you. And you're afraid that's just going to be the way it is, for the rest of your life. And I think you don't mind. Or, at least, you don't *think* you mind."

Kotler sipped his scotch again, and stared at the array of bottles on the bar back. A mirror there allowed him a view of the entire bar, from this vantage point, and he wondered vaguely if either he or Denzel had chosen this spot intentionally. Kotler watched as patrons filtered in from the hotel lobby, all ready to relax and have a nice evening chat. That's what he and Denzel were doing, wasn't it? Though Kotler doubted that most chats involved talk of combat training or FBI background checks.

The question was still hanging there. *Did* Kotler mind? He and Evelyn had been in love, that much Kotler knew and believed. But when she had moved to Houston, he hadn't even considered going with her. He had, in fact, been a bit relieved. Perhaps he had started to feel that he was at the end of a leash—limited in how far he could roam by the relationship he had with Evelyn. Or, as Denzel was suggesting, maybe it was something more.

Maybe he didn't want to endanger anyone, just by living

his life the way he always had.

"Evelyn and I had already come to a place where we were no longer together," Kotler said. "The events in Colorado just made it that much simpler to walk away, once she was safe."

"You miss her?" Denzel asked.

Kotler considered this. "Yes," he said, and sipped his scotch. "But I think I miss her in the way we always miss someone we once loved. Maybe it's primal. She was my mate—to my subconscious, maybe I thought of her as my property. Regardless of how well developed we become as a species, the baser parts of ourselves still think in terms of 'mine.' I think that's what drives us to miss someone, and to yearn for them, even if moving apart was mutually agreeable."

"How clinical," Denzel said, sipping from his own glass of amber now and shaking his head. "Kotler, you're probably the smartest guy I've ever met, but you can be an idiot about certain things. You've convinced yourself that it's best if you're alone. No real romantic attachments, beyond maybe a fling here and there. Maybe Evelyn wasn't the right one for you, or maybe she could have been. But I think you definitely need to wake up at some point. You live a pretty interesting life, I'll admit. But you don't have to live it alone."

Kotler laughed lightly, and shook his head. "I'm a terrible topic of conversation," he said. "Can we get back to the Atlantis Riddle?"

"Oh, it's a riddle now?" Denzel asked.

"It is to me," Kotler said. "I'm curious about all of this. I want to know *why* Gail and her Grandfather thought this would lead to Atlantis. And I want to know what Van Burren has discovered. Oh, and Rodham. I definitely want to know what he's hiding."

"You and me both," Denzel said. "And hopefully, in the morning, we'll find out."

Kotler slipped the key card into the reader on the door and entered his room, fumbling to find the light switch as he closed the door behind him. The lights flicked on, and Kotler blinked as he turned to discover someone seated in one of the plush chairs near the window.

The man—about 30 years old, dressed in a dark suit and reclined comfortably with one foot over his knee—waved a hand to Kotler, motioning for him to come closer.

On the table beside his chair was a pistol—a 9mm, if Kotler wasn't mistaken.

"Dr. Kotler," the man said. "I was beginning to think you and Agent Denzel were going on a bender."

"We had a lot to discuss," Kotler said cautiously. He was watching the man, reading him, trying to figure out what his intentions might be. Kotler found that in situations like this —and he'd been in far too many situations like this—it was best to remain cautious, confident, and somewhat aloof. Questions asked of his guest would be evaded. And any action Kotler might take could result in his being shot, which was never pleasant.

However, he could see that the man had no intention of shooting him, unless Kotler himself gave him cause. The man's body language suggested that he meant to imply a threat, but not carry one out unless forced to do so. He wanted to talk. And Kotler was fine with talking.

"What can I do for you?" Kotler asked.

"You've involved the FBI in on your search for the Edison Stone," the man said.

"It's more like the FBI brought me in," Kotler said. "I'm consulting with them in an investigation."

"Into Richard Van Burren," the man said.

Kotler made no reply. It was best to avoid confirmation, if possible. Whoever controlled all the facts would have the advantage in this sort of encounter.

"Please, Dr. Kotler. I know that Gail McCarthy brought you the stone her grandfather left her. And I know you've come here to retrieve the Edison Stone from Dr. Rodham. I have a vested interest in obtaining both of those stones, and the map that Van Burren is holding."

"Do you?" Kotler asked. "And who are you, exactly?"

The man considered. "You can call me Aslan."

"Aslan? As in the lion from the Narnia books? Analogous to Jesus?"

Aslan smiled. "I make no claims on deity. And I won't be anyone's savior. Call it an ironic code name, if it makes you feel better."

"Ironic," Kotler repeated. "Meaning you're more like the devil?"

"Ah, the devil," Aslan said, smiling and reaching lightly to touch the pistol beside him. "He comes in all sorts of forms, and maybe I'm one of them at that. I can tell you this, however. I will make your life a literal hell if you interfere with me getting my hands on those stones, and the map."

"I don't do well with threats, Aslan."

"I know that about you, actually," Aslan said, leaning back genially. "But let's consider it fair warning. Also," he reached into his pocket and took out a smartphone, "there's this."

Aslan tossed the phone to Kotler. When Kotler caught it he turned on the screen, and found that the photo app was open. There was a photo of Gail McCarthy, bound and gagged, her eyes filled with fear.

Kotler looked up at Aslan, who was smiling. It was clear now, Kotler realized, why the man felt no need to hold Kotler at gunpoint. He had Gail.

"Where is she?" Kotler asked.

"Somewhere safe," Aslan replied. "Narnia, perhaps! But don't worry. I have no intention of harming her, unless you let me down. And you won't let me down, Dr. Kotler. Because you're very good at what you do."

"And what is it you're asking me to do?" Kotler asked.

"First, I want you to procure the stones and the map. And while you're at it, I want you to divert the attention of Agent Denzel. I want him off chasing a ghost somewhere while we operate."

Kotler took this in. "And what then? What happens once you have the stones and the map?"

"Then? Well then you help me find Atlantis," Aslan smiled.

"It may not even be real. You realize that, of course."

"Oh it's real," Aslan said. "Van Burren has been sacking it for nearly half a century now. True, it may not be the *actual* Atlantis, for all I know. But Van Burren and McCarthy sure believed that it was. And now Van Burren has come to a place where he can't make any further progress without the stones. He's found something he needs to unlock, and those stones make the key."

"But you don't know where this lock is, do you?" Kotler asked.

Aslan shook his head, smiling. "No. I need an expert archeologist for that part. And a map."

Kotler shook his head. There was something about this that bugged him, but he couldn't quite make it click at the moment. There were too many factors. Plus the threat of a gun, and the threat against Gail McCarthy's life.

Aslan stood from the chair and smoothed his suit. He lifted the gun from the table and slipped it into a compact holster inside the flap of his coat. It disappeared there, without so much as a bulge.

"You're going to be tempted to talk to your FBI friend about this conversation," Aslan said. "I advise against it. If I suspect that the FBI knows about me, I will snuff the candle of our beautiful friend. Put him on a rabbit trail, Kotler. And get me those stones and the map. I'll be very generous, and give you 72 hours. Starting in the morning. You'll need a good night's sleep, after all."

"And Gail?" Kotler asked.

Aslan smiled as he walked past Kotler and opened the door to leave the room. "Keep the phone," Aslan said. "I'll be in touch."

He stepped out of the room and let the door close behind him.

Kotler made no move to follow. He stood perfectly still, staring at the photo of Gail McCarthy on the phone in his hand. Aslan had all the cards at the moment. He was running this show. For now.

What Kotler couldn't quite get out of his head, though, was that something was off about all of this. Who was Aslan? And why had he shown up here? It was clear he was confident and capable, and that he had a well-conceived plan. But then that opened a new line of questions for Kotler.

People who were working under their own agency, in situations like this, tended to send someone else to do their intimidating for them.

Which implied that Aslan wasn't in charge after all.

Kotler slipped the phone into his coat pocket, then locked and bolted the hotel door. He stripped and showered, and prepared for bed. The routine helped to relax him, which allowed his brain to tumble the questions and the data he already had over and over. He didn't have enough to come up with any real answers yet, but he was already organizing everything he knew in light of Aslan's appearance.

For now, Kotler needed sleep. Tomorrow morning he would have to work out the best way to betray Roland Denzel.

CHAPTER 6

BURLINGTON, VERMONT

"You seem tense," Denzel said as the two of them waited in the small breakfast area off of the hotel lobby. The bar where they'd spent the evening was just across the way, and Kotler had been watching two young women sitting and looking around in disbelief, apparently shocked that no one was taking their drink orders at eight in the morning.

He shook his head quickly and looked up at Denzel. They had each grabbed cups of coffee and muffins from the international breakfast bar. "Tired, I suppose," Kotler said, smiling. "I should have turned in earlier."

Denzel nodded, accepting this at face value.

Kotler felt like a heel.

The last thing he wanted to do was betray Denzel. And in fact, as Kotler understood the world, he knew that doing so would be a very bad idea. Denzel was a friend, it was true. But he was also an agent of a powerful organization, with resources that Kotler not only found personally useful, but which he'd be loath to have turned against him. He had already suffered under undue scrutiny from the FBI once, and that was far more than enough.

Aslan had given him 72 hours to produce both the stones and the map, upon threat to Gail's life. Kotler could feel the phone in his coat pocket—an uncomfortable weight he didn't wish to carry.

Seventy-two hours. That was all the time he had to figure a way out of this that did not jeopardize Gail's life, nor his relationship with Agent Denzel.

He suddenly had an idea.

"The courier is bringing the stone this morning, right?" he asked.

Denzel nodded. "He should be here in a couple of hours. What's up?"

"I wonder if I can find a hobby shop open at this time of day?"

Denzel shook his head. "I don't get it. What are you after?"

"Let's just say I'm pursuing a hobby." He rose from the table, and picked up the paper cup of coffee to carry with him. "Can I meet you here in two hours?"

Denzel was studying Kotler, clearly noting the odd behavior. Kotler tried to smile, to assure Denzel that things were fine, that this was just one of the quirks of an independent researcher with too many degrees and too much stimulation.

"Sure," Denzel said.

Kotler nodded. "I'll be back soon."

He turned and left Denzel in the breakfast area, and made his way out to the guest drop-off, in front of the hotel. He called up a car to take him into town, and on the way he felt the clench of his stomach and tried to keep his mind off of the expression on Denzel's face.

The look of suspicion.

Denzel watched Kotler leave, and sipped his coffee. His friend wasn't prone to absurd side trips. Not as far as Denzel had observed. Kotler had always been very focused, and meticulous about how he analyzed things.

Which meant that whatever he was up to was something he didn't want Denzel to know about. And that gave Denzel a twinge in his stomach.

Something was going on.

He finished his coffee, and had a hardboiled egg to go with his muffin. He then stood and went back to his room. He had intended to wait out the courier with Kotler, so they could leave immediately for Rodham's estate. But now he needed to check on something else.

His laptop was connected to the FBI database via a secure wireless signal, so he had no need for the hotel's wifi. He opened the files he'd pulled together for this case, and glanced through them.

Kotler's file was among them. In fact, it was the bulkiest file of the bunch, with reams of information about Kotler's career, his education, and his family. Denzel had pored over this material, trying to learn everything he could about Kotler's past, his motives and intentions, his habits. In one sense, Denzel was vetting a CI. In another, he was just trying to learn more about someone he now considered a friend.

All of the data Denzel had on Kotler actually told him very little about the man himself. It told a story of what Kotler had *done* in his life, but very little about *why he'd done it*. There was no family history on record that would fully explain why Kotler was who he was. In fact, he didn't have much family to speak of. His parents were both deceased, leaving Dan and a brother named Jeff. Jeff was married to a woman named Christina. And the two of them had a son—Alex Kotler—who was turning out to be quite the boy detective, according to what his records showed. Like uncle, like nephew, Denzel supposed.

The death of his parents could have been a catalyst for

who Kotler became. They died in a plane crash when Kotler was 13 years old. He and his brother had become wards of a man who had served as an assistant to Kotler's father—someone who had his own interesting background.

That was where most of the public information about Kotler stopped, until he was in his twenties, and already making a name for himself in research and academic circles. He went from anonymity to traveling the world as part of several dangerous expeditions, uncovering mysteries and buried truths in tombs and dig sites around the world. In public accounts, he had a knack for finding the oddest, quirkiest, most out of place history and solving all of the riddles surrounding it. And no one knew where the heck he'd come from.

He just seemed to appear in the world one day, by most accounts—a paragon of intelligence and curiosity, and someone with a remarkable talent for finding himself in odd and often dangerous scenarios.

Kotler was, by his very nature, a trouble magnet.

Denzel liked him. He trusted him. But he knew that something was going on with him right now, and Kotler wasn't being forthcoming about it.

Whatever it was, it had started some time between the two of them parting ways at the bar last night and meeting for coffee and breakfast just eight hours later.

Denzel picked up his room phone and dialed the front desk.

"Yes, this is Agent Denzel, with the FBI," he said, when the concierge answered. "I'm a guest in this hotel, along with one of our consultants. We're in an active investigation, and I was hoping I could take a look at some of your security camera footage."

Kotler left the hobby shop with a small bag containing modeling clay, quick-dry cement, and a few small containers of paint and pigment, along with several small brushes. He made sure he was obscured from view as he climbed into the car and was driven back to the hotel. He made his way quickly to his room, where he made preparations.

His phone rang.

Actually, as he went to answer it, he realized it was the phone that Aslan had given him last night. He inhaled and exhaled slowly, and answered the phone.

"Dan?" a woman's voice said.

"Gail," Kotler said. "Are you … are you alright?"

"There's a man here. He's holding the phone in front of me, and he told me to tell you that you're on speaker."

"I understand," Kotler said.

Proof of life. Aslan was sending him a reminder.

"He says they'll kill me," Gail said, her voice strained. "They want the stones."

"They?" Kotler asked. "Is there someone else there?"

Another voice came on the phone now, this time closer sounding. Kotler realized he was off of the speakerphone. "Don't worry about that, Dr. Kotler," Aslan's voice said. "The only person you have to worry about is me. I just wanted you to hear Ms. McCarthy's voice. So we're clear."

"We're clear," Kotler said. "I'm working on something now. A courier is bringing the first stone."

"Good. That just leaves you with the second, and the map. Oh, and 63 hours."

The line went dead, and the phone gave a beep to tell Kotler they had been disconnected. He looked at the display. "Unknown Number."

He went back to what he was doing. Time was going to get tight, and he had only one chance to pull this off.

There was a knock at the door, and Kotler fought the urge to groan. He took a deep breath and let it out slowly, then answered.

Denzel was standing in the hall, looking somber. He held up his phone, and Kotler saw a very clear photo of Aslan, taken by the camera at the end of the hall, several doors down from Kotler's room.

"Explain," Denzel said.

Kotler rubbed his forehead, and noticed his hands were covered in modeling clay. He held them up to show Denzel. "Hobby," he said. "Come in. This is going to take a bit."

He turned and went back to the table where he had prepared four small containers. They were sealable plastic crates, smaller by half than a shoebox, and perfect for shoving into a shoulder bag. Each contained a rectangle of modeling clay, level to the top, and each would fit together when one was turned upside down and pressed against the other.

"Molds," Kotler said.

"For what?" Denzel asked.

"For the stones. But beyond that, to save Gail McCarthy's life."

"Start explaining," Denzel said.

Kotler explained. He told Denzel about Aslan's visit, about Gail's kidnapping, about the phone call he'd just received. "I'll be honest, I hadn't counted on you showing up at my door with a picture of Aslan."

"I got suspicious," Denzel said. "I had the hotel pull up footage from last night, and I saw this guy. Did you know him before last night?"

Kotler shook his head. "No. And from what I've gathered, he doesn't work for Van Burren."

Denzel studied Kotler for a moment. "You should have told me," he said.

"You know I couldn't," Kotler replied. "Not without some way to ensure Gail's safety."

"Which is *my* job, Kotler."

Kotler nodded. He used one of the hotel towels to wipe

his hands. "You're right. No. You're right. I didn't handle this well. I'm not used to having someone to turn to for this sort of thing. I was trying to puzzle out how to find Gail."

Denzel studied him, then shook his head. "I was actually planning to arrest you, and now I just want to know what the tubs of clay are for."

"I'm going to create replicas of the stones to give to Aslan. To buy some time."

"Replicas? Will that work?"

Kotler shrugged. "I'm not certain. But I don't believe Aslan is an expert in any of this. I don't believe he will know the difference. I don't think he's even *seen* these stones."

"And what makes you think that?" Denzel asked.

"Because he's *wrong* somehow. He's *off*. I haven't quite put it together, but I don't think he knew anything about any of this before he was hired to come here. He was well informed —he knew a lot. But it was surface information. The sort of thing he might learn from someone who really is in charge."

"The 'they' that Gail mentioned on the phone?" Denzel asked.

"He picked up immediately after that. He doesn't want me knowing that he's working for someone else. He wants to keep me as ignorant as possible."

Denzel stared at Kotler, who was seated at the hotel desk, which had been turned into a workbench for the molds. Denzel shook his head. "Kotler, my training tells me that I shouldn't trust you."

"I understand," Kotler said. "I kept this from you. I would have kept it from you the whole time."

"But I know you. Well enough, anyway. This is what you do. You have a history for this sort of thing."

"Well, maybe a little," Kotler smiled.

Denzel shook his head. "Ok. Listen, we can't do it like this again. Got it? You tell me. That's the rule. Otherwise ..."

He didn't finish, but Kotler understood.

"What about the phone?" Denzel asked.

Kotler handed him the phone that Aslan had given him. "He wants me to keep it on me at all times. I'm pretty sure he's tracking it. I don't think we could send it to anyone to trace."

"We may not have to," Denzel said. "If we can duplicate the sim card, I can send it back with the courier, have my people dig into it."

Kotler thought about this. "There's a mobile phone dealer a block from here. They should have a way to scan and duplicate that sim card. Can you call ahead, convince them to help us? I'd have to move fast, in case Aslan really is tracking me."

"I'll set something up," Denzel said.

His own phone rang, and Denzel answered. When he hung up he said, "The courier is here."

"Bring him up," Kotler said. "This will actually be easier to pull off, now that you're onboard."

"Just out of curiosity, how were you planning to do this with me around?"

Kotler smiled. "Well, if I'm being honest, I hadn't worked out a plan just yet. So I'm kind of glad you found me out before I had to start improvising."

CHAPTER 7

HABBERSHAM ABBEY, VERMONT

DENZEL HAD MANAGED TO CONVINCE THE MANAGER OF the mobile phone store to let Kotler stroll in, walk straight into the back room, and hand the phone over for a very quick scan and duplication of the sim card. It took a few minutes, and Kotler had to admit he was worried about Aslan picking up on what was happening. If this phone really was being monitored and traced, Kotler's current location could give away the plan entirely.

Once the sim was copied, however, Kotler was able to get out of there in just a few seconds. Denzel had arranged for the FBI courier to stick around and take the sim to the closest Bureau offices, so the tech team could start digging into its data and history.

Kotler met with Denzel just outside of the shop, and the two of them walked for a few minutes until they came to their rental car. They were on the road to Habbersham Abby in moments.

Denzel had been carrying a small case, which contained the Atlantis Stone—a nomenclature that Denzel wasn't too thrilled about, but which he accepted without much debate.

This was the real stone. The fake one was currently curing under a hotel blow dryer, rigged to pass hot air into the mold and over the quick-dry cement. They had moved the operation to Denzel's room, in case Kotler got another visit from Aslan.

Kotler would paint the tarnished gold markings when he returned to the hotel. He had mixed a combination of pigments in with the clay to give the fake stones the right color and tone, along with the slight natural marbling of the stone, and he hoped that once everything was done they would have a replica that could fool the inexpert eye that Kotler was counting on from Aslan. It would buy them time to find Gail, he hoped.

That was one third of the equation. The second third would be making a copy of the Edison Stone, without Rodham knowing it. Kotler and Denzel discussed a number of possible scenarios and distractions, but in the end they would have to improvise. All Kotler needed was a few seconds to make the mold. He had the two small crates of clay in his shoulder bag, along with a camera and some equipment he would claim was necessary to 'examine' the Edison stone.

"This is never going to work in a million years," Denzel said. "And I'll probably be fired or worse, just for helping you."

"You say that every time we do something illegal," Kotler said, smiling.

"Not illegal," Denzel said quickly. "There's no law against making a clay mold of someone's property, as far as I can tell."

"A gray area indeed," Kotler nodded solemnly.

They arrived at Habbersham Abbey, and were greeted immediately by Rodham's butler. "This way, sirs," the butler intoned, his voice resonant and stern.

They followed him away from the drive, and down a stone path which led to an outbuilding about a hundred yards from the main house. It was surrounded by ash and birch trees, with a smattering of pine here and there. Large stones, both natural and carved, lined the rear perimeter, creating a wall of sorts that separated the manicured grounds of the estate from the more wild and untamed forest growth beyond.

This building, from Kotler's perspective, must have at one time been some sort of mill—though Kotler wasn't sure what this region would have been known for. The building had been remodeled and converted at some point in its history, and as they entered it became clear that it was now a personal museum of sorts.

Rodham was standing within, his hands folded behind his back. The butler spoke up as they entered. "Agent Denzel and Doctor Kotler, sir."

"Thank you Krantz," Rodham said. "That will be all."

Krantz left them then, retreating to some spot where he could be within listening distance, Kotler had no doubt, should his master call.

"Dr. Rodham," Denzel said. He lifted the case containing the stone. "We have held up our side of the bargain. Would you care to examine the stone?"

Rodham's eyes were glued to the case. He nodded involuntarily, and tilted his head toward a large, oak door. "This way to the clean room," he said.

They followed Rodham through the door, which was locked by a very sophisticated biometric panel. Rodham entered a code, and placed his palm on a scanner, then said, "Rosebud."

Kotler smiled. "Citizen Kane?"

"I found it poetic," Rodham said, not bothering to glance back. "The system is tuned to my voice alone, by the by."

A warning, Kotler realized, that they would not be able to enter just because they knew the magic word.

They followed Rodham down a corridor that ended at a large, glass door. Again Rodham entered a code, but this time the door merely clicked, and he was able to push it open with no trouble.

A gust of air hit them as they entered, followed by a mist from the ceiling, and the vacuum pull of air being sucked downward—a negative pressure environment. The mist covered them instantly, but it wasn't wet. It was actually a fine powder, which was sucked away into the floor, without leaving a trace.

Kotler recognized it. Each particle was actually a negatively charged bit, which would cling to microparticles on their clothing, loose hairs, flakes of skin—anything that was small enough to flake off of them unnoticed while in the clean room. The 'vacuum' had been more than air, then. It was a flow of positively charged air particles snatching up the negatively charged bits along with their microscopic cargo. An efficient way to clean your average human.

Kotler had encountered technology like this in national archives, but had never seen it in personal use. It spoke to Rodham's great wealth.

Rodham led them now to a room that contained several highly polished wooden boxes arranged on shelves that covered every wall from floor to ceiling. He went to a rolling library ladder, moved it into position, and climbed to the third row from the top. He pried a small box out of its cubby, and brought it down to place on an examining table.

He took three sets of lint-free examination gloves from a dispenser under the table, and gave them to Denzel and Kotler.

The two exchanged glances as they pulled on the gloves.

If Rodham was this cautious, it was going to be very difficult to get the stone away from him long enough to duplicate it.

At Rodham's urging, Denzel placed the case containing the Atlantis stone on the examining table. Rodham reached for it, but Denzel said, "We need to see the Edison stone first."

Rodham looked at him, annoyed. "You see nothing until I examine your stone."

"Then we'll compromise," Denzel said.

He opened the case, and showed the stone to Rodham for a brief moment. Rodham reached for it reflexively, and Denzel clamped the case shut again.

"We want to examine your stone, closely," Denzel said. "And while we do, you can examine ours."

Rodham had an expression of disgust on his face, and Kotler could see the man was fighting his anger. He wanted something, and someone in authority was denying it to him. Or rather, was making his access to it *conditional*. Kotler knew that Rodham wasn't accustomed to being limited in this way.

There were a few tense seconds before Rodham finally gave a curt nod.

He stepped aside and allowed Kotler to move to the wooden box. Kotler donned the exam gloves, and carefully lifted the lid to the box, revealing the stone set in a molded felt inset.

He glanced at Denzel, who gave a brief nod.

"Ok, Dr. Rodham, if you'll step over here we'll take a look at the stone that Dr. Kotler and I brought."

Rodham moved somewhat reluctantly but his interest in the Atlantis Stone overpowered his urge to keep his eyes on the Edison stone at all times. Kotler had already busied himself with removing several devices and objects from his bag, as part of his 'examination' of the stone.

Now he removed the two tubs of clay, and while Rodham was peering through a jeweler's loupe at the Atlantis stone, Kotler pushed the Edison Stone into the clay, and quickly brought the other tub up and over, making impressions of both sides.

He let this sit for just a moment—a tense few seconds that he counted down as if waiting for a bomb to go off. He then pulled the tubs apart, removed the stone, and then placed lids on the two tubs before shoving them back into his bag. He used a polishing cloth to quickly rub away any clay residue from the stone, and was holding it as if getting a better look when Rodham turned and removed the loop from his eye.

"Remarkable," he said, a genuine smile on his face. "The markings, the indentations, the gold filament—it's a perfect mate for my Edison Stone!"

He turned back to the Atlantis stone, and gently lifted it from its place in the foam interior of the case. He turned it in his gloved hands, examining it from every angle. And then he looked from Denzel to Kotler.

"Should we … should we bring them together?"

Kotler smiled. "Dr. Rodham, if we didn't I would leave here a very disappointed man."

Rodham actually grinned, which was so counter to everything Kotler and Denzel had experienced from the man so far, it was all Kotler could do to keep from laughing out loud.

Kotler picked up the Edison Stone and placed it on a felt pad that Rodham had hastily brought from a narrow drawer in the table.

Rodham then placed the Atlantis stone on the pad, in close proximity, but not touching the Edison stone.

He looked at Kotler, who nodded, and then like a child

cautiously testing a frog to see if it would leap, Rodham nudged the stones together.

There was an audible *click* as the two stones came close to each other, and then suddenly connected without Rodham's help.

"They must contain magnets," Kotler whispered, awed.

Rodham carefully lifted the combined stones, turning the now square object in his hands, over and over.

Kotler took out a camera, and Rodham placed the stones on the felt pad once more. Kotler took photographs from several angles, including numerous closeups of the seams, the combined filaments, and the patterns of markings.

Rodham turned the object over, and Kotler repeated the process. They came away with dozens of detailed photos.

"I'd like to do a deeper scan," Kotler said. "Looks like magnetic resonance imaging may be out, if there are magnets inside of these stones. But there are other means. I have access to deep scan technology that could give us a look inside of these."

"The technology you used in the Viking discovery," Rodham nodded.

"Exactly," Kotler said. "Would you allow me to take your stone for scanning and further testing?"

Rodham looked at Kotler for a long moment. Kotler could sense hesitation and wariness, but it was plain in Rodham's body language that the man was eager to know more. And then, apparently, he came to some internal decision.

"I will allow it, but I will accompany you."

Kotler and Denzel exchanged glances. Denzel's lips were pursed in a slight frown, but he nodded.

It was less than ideal for Rodham to tag along, but Kotler had been prepared for the eventuality. He and Denzel had discussed it on the drive in, and Kotler had even taken things a step further by calling ahead to the labs he used in Manhattan. The same labs, in the basement of the American Museum of Natural History, where Dr. Coelho had conducted his initial research into Viking artifacts from the Pueblo dig site. Kotler had privileges there, and he had full access to the new scanning technology.

Kotler had made arrangements for Rodham and Agent Denzel to have access to the labs, while Kotler was there. It would actually serve as a nice cover—something for Aslan to see as proof that Kotler was still playing by the rules.

It also gave Kotler and Denzel a way to get everything back to Manhattan where, presumably, Richard Van Burren was keeping the map—the third and final piece that Kotler was supposed to retrieve.

He had no idea how to even find the map, much less liberate it from Van Burren. But he still had nearly two days to figure it out. And in the meanwhile, perhaps delivering the stones would buy him some time.

They made arrangements with Rodham, who would personally bring the stones to the museum that very afternoon. Then Kotler and Denzel left, climbing back into the rental car and speeding away to the hotel, where they would gather the rest of their things before heading to the local airport to catch a small plane back to the city.

"You got it?" Denzel asked.

Kotler patted his bag. "I got it. I'll use it to make a duplicate of the stone once we're back in New York."

Denzel let out a breath. "Is this going to work?" he asked.

Kotler said nothing. Because he didn't know.

CHAPTER 8

AMERICAN MUSEUM OF NATURAL HISTORY, MANHATTAN

RODHAM ARRIVED WITH A DRIVER AND AN ASSISTANT IN tow. The driver looked to be ex-military, from Kotler's perspective. He had a tight and muscled frame, and he moved with precision.

So not just a driver, Kotler mused. *A bodyguard.*

The assistant, on the other hand, was a slight and petite African American woman who was in no way as meek as her size would suggest. She took charge immediately upon entering the labs, arranging for an office space for Dr. Rodham's personal use, and alerting museum staff that Dr. Rodham was not to be approached or disturbed during his examination of the stones.

"Jeez," Denzel said. "You'd think the guy owned the place."

"Doesn't matter," Kotler said. "As long as he's allowing us to scan his stone alongside ours, we can tolerate a little drama."

"For now," Denzel replied ominously, and Kotler stifled a grin.

They used one of the clean rooms to set up the scanners,

THE ATLANTIS RIDDLE 95

and placed the stones on an examination table. They looked incongruous sitting amongst the high tech instruments and tablet computers—these ancient stones of unknown origin, nestled amongst 21st century technology.

This room was kept dust and particle free by a constant negative charge in the air. The equipment had been grounded to points outside of the room, and everything had been sterilized. Most of the precautions taken were a bit of overkill, considering both of these stones had been handled numerous times by who knew whom, over the past century. But these were standard protocols, and they helped add to the seriousness of the whole affair, which Kotler knew would make Rodham feel more at ease. He was a man who dealt in perceptions—and that attitude extended to items in his possession as much as to his own person.

Kotler turned to one of the machines that stood in a bridge-like arch over the table. "This is the Sonic Resonance Scanner with Laser Detection and Ranging. SRS-LIDAR, if we need to fall back on acronyms. It's a hybrid scanner that uses sonic imaging technology to penetrate the material being scanned, while LIDAR maps the surface in great detail. The data is parsed and combined so that each internal ping from the sonic scanning is correlated with whatever surface details are scanned by the laser."

"I've read about this," Rodham said, nodding. "I've wanted to see it up close for some time."

"There are only three of them on the planet at the moment," Kotler said. "And, incidentally, one in space. One of these was modified and loaded into the probe that is currently making its way to Mars."

Rodham scowled. "Can we just get on with the scan?"

Kotler nodded. He'd geeked out too much—a common problem when he started talking about new technologies or new discoveries.

He activated the scanner, and they stepped back as it moved under its own power, rolling with large, pillared legs on either side of the exam table, emitting a grid of laser light that took in the surface details of the stones.

They scanned each stone separately, both top and bottom, and then connected them and repeated the process.

The data they received was stunning.

"I don't believe it," Kotler said, staring at the screen. The scanning equipment and computers had combined everything into a 3D model that they could animate, allowing them to move the virtual stones around on screen, taking them apart and putting them back together—and most importantly, peeking inside.

The stones were each hollow, and within their small caverns was a series of peaks and valleys—a definite carved pattern that looked a bit like a maze. At key points there were spots of white, glowing from the darkness of the stone interiors.

"What are those?" Denzel asked, bending to look closer.

"Ferrous material," Kotler said. "Magnets. Natural magnets. From the data, I'd say they're nickel-iron, which makes them all the more fascinating."

"Why?" Denzel asked.

This time it was Rodham who spoke, and for once his voice was quiet and a bit awed as he peered closer at the scans of the stones. "That material was only found in meteorites and comets."

Denzel blinked. "You're saying these stones come from *space?* "

"Initially at least," Kotler smiled. "They aren't proof of alien life, Agent Mulder."

Denzel made a face and shook his head unconsciously. When he and Kotler had first met, Denzel was partnered with an Agent named Scully, and the two had been quick to negate the 'X-Files' references. By now it must be habit.

Kotler continued. "What it means is that whoever crafted these stones was using meteorite or other extraterrestrial materials, probably after finding fragments in an impact. What interests me, though, is the complete lack of a seam." Kotler examined the physical stones directly, picking them up in gloved hands, turning them to look closer. "The gold filament," Kotler said. "It forms language patterns, but if you look closely it also seals a cap piece onto each stone. See?" He held the stones out, indicating the filaments.

Rodham stepped in before Denzel had a chance to take a look, and he took the stones in his own hands, holding them close to his face, peering through his glasses at the intricate work. "My word," he whispered. "All these years, and I never noticed it."

The gold filament sealed the caps in place, that was certain. But what about the patterns within the stones themselves? Kotler turned back to the display, and rotated the stones on screen, watching to see how the internal patterns lined up.

"The magnets are at very specific points," Kotler said. "Whoever made these was making a very sophisticated key. To them, it may well have seemed like magic. But the effect is pretty sophisticated. Going by just these patterns, I'd say there are thousands, maybe millions of permutations. A combination lock, of sorts. Not only would you need both stones together, you would need to align them just right to unlock … well, *something*."

"Something," Denzel said. "The something we'll only be able to find with Van Burren's map."

Kotler glanced at Rodham when Denzel said Van Burren's name, looking for evidence that he might know the man.

Rodham was staring at the stones, which he'd been doing all this time. But Kotler caught the slight pause, the stiffening that said he'd heard Van Burren's name. He recognized it. He knew Van Burren.

Denzel picked up on this as well.

"Dr. Rodham, are you acquainted with Richard Van Burren?"

Rodham continued to study the stones, using them as a prop to keep from facing the Agent. It was a classic diversion tactic, Kotler knew. He was hiding behind those stones, for the moment.

"We have a passing acquaintance," Rodham said. "He has contributed to some of my political campaigns."

"And procured some of the pieces in your collection?" Kotler asked.

Rodham's immediate response was a tightening in his jaw, but he said aloud, "I obtain all of my pieces legally."

"Meaning that you're aware of Van Burren's smuggling operation," Denzel said.

Rodham was flustered now. He looked up from the stones, involuntarily, and Kotler could read the slight panic in his eyes.

He was lying about his relationship with Van Burren, and about how he obtained at least *some* of the objects in his collection. "I assure you, I was not," he said to Denzel, cold indignation in his voice.

But again, this was a lie. Kotler detected the sudden but slight change in octave, which indicated that Rodham had been flustered by this turn in the conversation, and was attempting to recover and mask his real reaction.

"Dr. Rodham," Kotler said, "Van Burren is the subject of Agent Denzel's investigation. I'm sure that if you cooperate," he glanced at Denzel, who nodded slightly, "you could receive some kind of deal. Protection."

"Immunity?" Rodham asked.

Denzel spoke up this time. "That depends largely on how much assistance you're willing to give," he said.

Rodham looked from one to the other of them. "Why do I suddenly feel this little field trip was a setup from the beginning?"

Kotler shook his head. "We are legitimately inserted in the stones, believe me. But Van Burren is dangerous, and his operation has gone almost completely unchecked for decades. If you help us, we can stop him. And that will look very good for you."

That had Rodham's attention. "This could be made public," Rodham said, rather than ask.

Denzel answered, "My investigation will eventually be a matter of public record. The reports haven't been written yet."

The implication was clear. Rodham could be painted as just another bad guy, or as the hero. The latter would play well with his plans.

Kotler watched as the scenarios played out for Rodham. He was a very intelligent man, despite his elitist tendencies. He knew the implications of all of this.

He sniffed. "Very well, what do I need to do?"

"Well, for starters we will take the Edison stone into our possession," Denzel said. "As part of our investigation."

Rodham didn't like this, but he nodded.

"And then we need you to help us retrieve something from Van Burren," Kotler said.

Rodham looked at Kotler. "What would that be?"

"A map," Kotler said. "We have to get our hands on a map Van Burren has in his possession. And we need to do it within the next 24 hours."

Rodham considered this. "He always meets with me when I call," he said. "I can arrange to meet at his home."

"He won't think that's suspicious?" Denzel asked.

Rodham shook his head. "We meet there often. He has scrambling devices to prevent anyone from using recording or transmitting technology. You will not be able to monitor our conversation." This last was said with just the faintest smirk. He was taking satisfaction that in this, at least, he still had some control.

Kotler almost hated to disappoint him. Almost.

"That's what we expected," Kotler said. "And it's fine. We need access anyway. We'll be going in with you."

CHAPTER 9

RICHARD VAN BURREN'S ESTATE

THEY ARRIVED BY LIMO, WHICH DENZEL THOUGHT WAS a bit unnecessary, and Kotler thought was perfect.

"It will allay suspicion until the last moment," Kotler said. "Van Burren would expect our good Dr. Rodham to arrive in his customary style." Kotler nodded toward Rodham, who was sitting quietly, staring out of the window. His body language indicated he was tense and unsure, but he was keeping this in check.

Denzel sighed. "Kotler, I've noticed that you always have a way to justify little bits of luxury."

Kotler smiled. "Spend enough time crawling through tombs and caves and you'll gain a much greater appreciation for every fine moment you can manage."

The driver opened Rodham's door first, and Rodham stepped out and to the side as Denzel and Kotler followed.

"I am uncertain how Van Burren will react to the two of you accompanying me," Rodham said.

"He and I have already met," Kotler said. "And he'll likely know who Agent Denzel is from background research. I expect his reaction will be extreme suspicion, and a willingness to throw you under the bus at the first opportunity."

Rodham reacted visibly to this last bit.

"Don't worry," Kotler said. "You have your deal, remember?"

"As I understand it, the deal is contingent upon your getting Van Burren's map."

"There is that," Denzel said. "Let's go."

They entered a foyer, where they were greeted by one of Van Burren's people. From there they were shown into what looked like a conference room on the main floor. Van Burren ran his side of the business out of his home, it seemed. Or, Kotler mused, this was for his *other* business—a safe place in his own home to meet with smugglers and thieves, free of any fear of wire tapping or surveillance. As Kotler looked around the room, he noticed the door frames were thicker than one typically saw in home construction, by a few inches.

Armor plating, Kotler thought. This room was ready for conflict.

Though there was a large conference table dominating the room, surrounded by executive chairs, the three of them opted to remain standing. Kotler could sense Denzel's unease —he had clearly noted the armored walls, and like Kotler was probably wondering what *else* Van Burren had packed into this room.

Rodham was a miserable wreck, from Kotler's perspective. The man was standing stiff and tense, his hands clasped behind his back and his chin high. But it was a front. He was as tense as Denzel—maybe even more so. Kotler noted the slight clenching of his jaw, the rigid expression, the slight fidget as Rodham shifted his weight from side to side at measured intervals.

It was several long minutes before Van Burren entered

the room, along with two large, muscled, and well-armed security personnel.

"Dr. Kotler," Van Burren said, his voice all drawl and hospitality, but for that slight edge of tension. Van Burren looked at Rodham first, then at Denzel. "And you're the FBI agent," he said.

Denzel showed his badge and said, "FBI Special Agent Denzel. We'd like to ask you a few questions, Mr. Van Burren."

Van Burren nodded and then looked to Rodham. "Lester, I'm at a loss as to why you would bring these men into my home without first asking me. I thought we had a much better relationship than that." There was a sort of *tut-tut* tone to Van Burren's voice that made Rodham cringe slightly. It was subtle, but Kotler picked up on it, and realized just how afraid Rodham was of the man.

But therein was the problem—Rodham was supposed to be the one in power. That was the fantasy he'd built around himself. It was how he had internally justified bringing Kotler and Denzel to Van Burren's home, even though he was clearly under Denzel's power as well. All of these little upsets to Rodham's delusion were making it difficult for him to maintain his facade. He was cracking under the pressure of cognitive dissonance.

"Mr. Van Burren," Denzel said, "I'd like to ask you a few questions, if you don't mind. We've been following some of your activities over the past several years. It seems your name comes up fairly often when the subject of antiquities is raised. Particularly if there's some question as to where those antiquities come from."

Van Burren shrugged. "It's no secret that I operate a side import business," he said.

"And I'm certain you can provide paperwork for every-thing you .. *import*," Kotler said.

"Of course, Dr. Kotler. I'm in business, after all. I make sure to keep thorough records, and everything is *always* in order."

This game could go on for quite a while, and Kotler could see that Denzel was sharing his impatience with all of it. "Van Burren," Kotler said. "Do you have a map to Atlantis?"

There was a moment of stunned silence after Kotler asked the question, and he could see from the corner of his eye that Denzel was flinching and Rodham was staring in open-mouthed disbelief.

But he kept his attention focused on Van Burren, who was oddly calm.

"What a silly question," Van Burren replied.

"We have the stones," Kotler said. "Both of them. With us."

Now Van Burren was reacting without his calm and calculated demeanor. "You have them here?" he asked, his eyes widening slightly.

"And we're prepared to allow you access to them, in exchange for access to the map."

This was a dangerous play, and Denzel hadn't entirely agreed to it beforehand. Kotler needed Van Burren to reveal that map, at least long enough for him to get a photo of it, if not lay hands on it directly. Gail's life depended on them delivering the stones and the map within the next 24 hours.

Time had wound down faster than Kotler would have liked. He had no desire to jeopardize Denzel's case against Van Burren, but he knew that Denzel would not want to risk Gail's life, either.

It was a fine balance to strike, however—getting hold of the map without giving Van Burren any sort of out from the smuggling charges.

Van Burren was studying Kotler. "You're aware that I could just have my men *take* the stones?"

"That wouldn't be a smart play," Denzel said. He was simply standing, slightly to the right and in front of Van Burren, and hadn't so much as made a move toward the weapon tucked into a holster inside his coat. But he still read as enough of a threat that the two beefcake security guards involuntarily stepped forward.

Van Burren held up a hand to make them step back. He was a man who was as accustomed to violence as he was to his extravagant lifestyle, but even he knew that directly confronting the FBI would only bring hell down on his head. Kotler watched as Van Burren calculated his next move, taking in all of the facts of the situation, weighing options. He came to a conclusion.

"Alright," Van Burren said, eyeing each of them. "If you show me the stones, I'll show you the map."

Kotler glanced at Denzel, who nodded, and then Kotler slipped the shoulder bag off and placed it on the table. He opened the bag to reveal the two stones, set in foam insets that were sheathed in felt. The entire display was covered by a sheet of clear plexiglass, offering a view of the stones without allowing instant access to them.

Kotler removed the plexiglas cover so that the stones were completely unobscured by reflections from the lights above the table.

Van Burren peered into the case, his eyes alight. "It's been a long time," he said, involuntarily reaching toward the Atlantis stone.

Kotler quickly placed the cover back on top, and closed the case. He slung the whole thing back over his shoulder.

Van Burren started at him, a slight expression of annoyance actually breaking the collected facade for an instant. "I'd like to actually examine them closer," he said.

"We'll give you that chance," said Denzel. "Plus some of the research we've collected. After we're allowed to examine the map."

Van Burren looked again at Agent Denzel, as if appraising him.

He turned to one of his men and whispered something Kotler couldn't make out. The man turned and left the room quickly.

"It will be a few minutes," Van Burren said.

They waited, and the silence was definitely tense.

Kotler watched everyone, studying, seeing who was stressed and who had it together. Rodham was a wreck, but Denzel and Van Burren were pure stone. The remaining security guard may as well have been a statue himself, for all the emotion or movement he was showing.

After nearly twenty tense minutes, the first guard returned carrying a flat, locked case.

He placed this on the conference table and stepped back. Van Burren stepped forward, placing his thumb on a fingerprint reader in the case. There was a beep, and a small, green LED came on.

Now Van Burren entered a numerical code, and a second LED came on.

Finally he pressed in two tabs on either side of the case and opened the lid, exposing the contents inside.

Within the case was the map, wedged between two sheets of clear plexiglass, which was sealed on all sides by silicone. The map had been remarkably well preserved, and it was clear that Van Burren valued it highly.

Kotler placed the case with the stones back on the table, and opened it up for Van Burren to once again peer inside. The effect was less dramatic than Van Burren's biometric briefcase, but it had no less impact. Van Burren fairly rushed to the case, bending once again to see inside.

He reached for the Atlantis stone.

"Not so fast," Kotler said. "Looking is free. Touching will cost you."

Van Burren looked up, a small smile on his face. "And what is the price of fondling ancient stones these days, Dr. Kotler?"

"Photos," Kotler said. "I want to document the map."

Van Burren stood up straight, his expression becoming stern. "Not under any circumstances," he said.

Kotler shook his head. "Then there's no deal, Van Burren. The stones for the map—that's the only way."

Van Burren considered this. "And what about the charges our good friend Agent Denzel is trying to bring up against me? Surely a chance to examine my little map is worth a bit of immunity?"

"And why would you need immunity, Van Burren?" Denzel asked. "You're innocent, aren't you?"

"A man in my line of work can't afford to rely on either the presumption or the perception of innocence," Van Burren chuckled. "He has to have it in writing."

Denzel exchanged another look with Kotler, then sighed. "Everyone wants immunity," he said, now glancing at Rodham, who was all but cringing from across the room. "OK, Van Burren, here's the deal—we get full access to the map and anything tied to it, and you get full access to the stones. Immunity is contingent upon cooperation. I'm looking to shut down a smuggling network that I believe you're part of, if not in charge of. So we'll talk about the prospect of protecting you, if you're willing to bring down the rest of the network."

Again Van Burren chuckled. "Well isn't that somethin'?" he asked. "I mean, were I the one in charge of this 'smuggling network'—not saying I am, mind you—it would be downright foolish of me to help shut it down, don't you

think? It might be a sizable portion of my income and interests. It might be something too big to shut down at any rate."

"It might," Denzel said, nodding. "But how sure are you
that it won't come down? At least this way you stand a
chance of staying out of prison."

Van Burren smiled, and was about to respond to this,
when there was a sudden explosion of noise and activity
outside the room.

The double doors to the conference room had stood open
the entire time they'd been inside, and now Van Burren's two
men rushed through those doors to investigate the noise.

There was a quick burst of gunfire—semi automatic
weapons, from what Kotler could determine—and both
guards flailed backward, twisting and falling face first to the
floor.

Both were dead.

Denzel already had his weapon out and was pulling
Rodham to cover behind the conference table and chairs.

Kotler had no weapon, and suddenly felt naked without
one, but he too ducked for cover, grabbing Van Burren and
pulling him down beside him.

They had barely hidden themselves when two figures
rushed through the door of the conference room, weapons
sweeping.

"Down! Stay down!" the men shouted, and one punctu-
ated the command by firing a burst into the wall above
Denzel's head. The bullets pierced the wooden facade,
revealing the steel plating that Kotler had suspected was
there.

Everyone stayed down.

Kotler peered over the edge of the table as the two men
grabbed the cases containing the map and the stones, then
started backing out of the room.

"Like hell!" Van Burren said, suddenly reaching up and

under the edge of the table, pushing a small panel that released and revealed a 9mm handgun.

He raised this quickly and squeezed off three rounds, striking one of the men in the shoulder, and then in the head.

The other turned, and without a glance at his fallen comrade he raised his weapon and put three bursts in Van Burren's chest.

Van Burren let out a strange '*oof*' noise, and then fell forward, slamming his head on the table before rolling to the side. Kotler could see instantly that the man was dead.

The intruder grabbed the map case from his partner, and raced from the room ahead of a barrage of shots from Denzel.

"We have to get that map!" Kotler shouted. He stooped and picked up the 9mm from Van Burren, and then he and Denzel raced to the door of the conference room, checking before running through.

The hall leading into this part of Van Burren's home was a complete disaster. There had been a brief but effective firefight as the men had burst in, gunned down Van Burren's staff, and made their way directly to the conference room.

And now this corridor was empty, save for the bodies of Van Burren's staff.

"This way!" Denzel shouted, and Kotler followed him through the chaos and out through the front door of the mansion.

Outside, the man with the cases was loading them into a black SUV with no plates. He had two other men with him, and as he climbed into the SUV the others covered him by laying down a *lot* of gunfire.

Denzel and Kotler ducked back into the house, waiting it out, and as soon as there was a break the two of them spun around the door frame and opened fire.

Too late.

The SUV was already speeding away, halfway up the drive, and in seconds they were on the road leading away from Van Burren's estate.

Denzel got on his mobile phone and called in the incident, arranging for local police to be on the lookout, and for paramedics to be sent to Van Burren's estate.

When he was done, Denzel turned and kicked a small boulder that lay innocently in the landscaping just outside of the front entrance.

"Dammit!" he raged.

Kotler knew exactly how he felt.

CHAPTER 10

RICHARD VAN BURREN'S ESTATE

POLICE AND PARAMEDICS WERE TENDING THE SCENE. There were FBI agents there as well, combing through everything they could find. So far they had determined that there were cameras all throughout the house, and the agents were studying footage from these now, trying to find some clue as to who had initiated this assault.

Denzel and Kotler searched other rooms of the house, hoping to find clues to what might have been on the map.

"I'm seeing a lot of dead ends," Denzel said, after they had combed through Van Burren's personal office.

"Whoever did this was efficient," Kotler mused as he thumbed through a stack of ledgers. "They knew the layout of this place."

"You're right," Denzel said, nodding. "They came in knowing exactly where Van Burren's people would be. And they knew we were in the conference room, with the stones and the map."

"So they have access to the security system," Kotler mused.

They left the office and found the agents on scene, telling

them their suspicions. After a brief search, they found a transmitter wired into the security feed—from within the home.

"This took serious planning," Kotler said, stooping to trace a small, unobtrusive wire that ran from the security panel and into an outlet, where it tapped into the house's back up power. "Look at this," Kotler said. "There's dust on this wire. It's been here for a long while. Whoever set it up had to have had access along with intimate knowledge of this place."

"Someone on the housing staff, maybe?"

Kotler shrugged, uncertain. He stood and looked into the security panel again. "Whoever it was, they've been waiting for this opportunity," he said. "This wasn't a coincidence. Somehow, someone knew we would be here with the stones. And they waited until the exact moment that Van Burren revealed the map."

"How?" Denzel asked. "Who could have known we'd be here, much less that we'd have the stones with us?"

Kotler suspected he knew, and was about to say so.

At that moment, the burner phone in Kotler's pocket rang. He looked up at Denzel, and then answered it.

"Well, I have to say, you did a fine job," said Aslan's voice.

"It was you," Kotler said, more confirmation than realization.

"I couldn't have done without you, Dr. Kotler. Thank you, truly."

"You went to a lot of trouble to set this up," Kotler said. "More time than I would have anticipated. Who was your inside man?"

"Now that would be telling," Aslan said, and Kotler could hear the man's smile over the phone. "But I will say that you're right. This plan has been in the works for a very long time, and you played into it perfectly. So be aware of that, Dr. Kotler. I plan very far ahead."

"What about Gail?" Kotler asked. "You have what you wanted. Will you let her go?"

"I already have," Aslan said. "She's back in her apartment, probably barricading herself in while she waits for the police to arrive. I keep my word."

"What an honorable thief and murderer you are," Kotler said.

Aslan chuckled. "One must have rules, if there's any hope for civilization."

"And now what?" Kotler asked. "You got what you were after, so why call?"

"Checking in," Aslan said casually. "Reminding you I'm here. Maybe I'm just trying to make a meaningful connection with you, Dr. Kotler."

"Well, in that case, why don't you meet up with me? I'm sure we'd have plenty to chat about."

Aslan laughed. "No, I don't think so. But you'll definitely be hearing from me again. I have need of your expertise."

"But you gave away your bargaining chip," Kotler reminded him.

"Oh her? Yes, she made for a nice bit of motivation. But I have other means of motivating you. Don't worry, I'll be in touch. And you can toss that phone now. I know you had the FBI duplicate the SIM card. It won't do much good."

With that, Aslan hung up.

Kotler turned to Denzel, and scowled. "Aslan. He let Gail go, but he made it clear this isn't over."

"He let her go? Wasn't she his leverage?"

"Yes," Kotler said. "But he implied he has more."

"I'll put people on Evelyn," Denzel said. "Just in case."

"And Eloi Coelho," Kotler said. "It's possible Aslan knows I visit him."

Denzel nodded. "So what's the play now? They made off with everything we had as a lead."

Kotler laughed lightly. "Well, not quite everything. They didn't get the stones at least."

Denzel looked at him, curious, then smiled as he realized what Kotler meant. "You switched them," he said. You brought the fake stones."

Kotler nodded. "It didn't seem prudent to bring the real thing into the lion's den."

Denzel chuckled. "Thank God for small victories. But what good does it do us? Without the map, aren't we just in the same boat?"

Kotler thought about this. "The security feeds don't cover the conference room, do they?"

"No," Denzel said. "Apparently Van Burren was too paranoid to video his own meetings."

"But the corridors outside of the conference room—they're covered?"

"Right," Denzel said. He led Kotler to the FBI's IT team, who were scanning footage, grabbing screenshots to use as evidence.

Kotler cycled through the screenshots until he found what he was looking for. "It doesn't look like we have the whole map," he said, "but there's enough here to reconstruct a large portion of it from both sides. There are half a dozen shots here that might show all the various pieces, if we can stitch them together."

Denzel turned to the IT lead. "Can you guys rebuild that map? Make it a single image that you can send to me?"

"Sure thing," the guy said. "It'll take maybe an hour."

"Good," Denzel said. "Text it to my phone." He rattled off his number, and then left the room with Kotler in tow.

"Back to Manhattan?" Kotler asked.

"We'll check in on your girlfriend, and then see what other leads we can dig up."

"I'm not even going to play the 'not my girlfriend' game with you," Kotler said.

Denzel grinned. "That's as much as admitting it."

Gail McCarthy was definitely shaken, though she looked to have come through the ordeal just fine, physically.

She was seated at the end of a large, polished dining table, with several screenshots spread out in front of her, along with an artist's rendering of Aslan, based on Kotler's description.

"Gail," Kotler said, "is there *anything* you can tell us that might help? Did you speak with Aslan?" He indicated the artist's sketch as he said this.

Gail shook her head. "No," she said. "They grabbed me and had my head covered the entire time. I heard some people talking from another room, but the only time I actually heard Aslan's voice was when he was talking to Dan and put me on the phone."

Denzel was taking a few notes, but looked up and asked, "You said they drove you somewhere. Do you have an idea of how long you were in the vehicle?"

"Not really," Gail said. "Maybe ten minutes. Fifteen at the most."

"So someplace close," Denzel said. "Do you recall any sounds? Smells?"

Gail shook her head. "Nothing," she said. "I'm sorry."

At this last she reached up and touched the side of her face, a self comforting gesture. "I can't believe I was so *stupid.*"

"Stupid?" Kotler asked. "How so?"

"When they knocked on my door, I thought it was odd. I wasn't expecting anyone. But I forgot to check the door camera before opening the door. They had me in seconds."

Kotler nodded. "That was a mistake, but that doesn't make you in any way responsible for what happened. You were abducted by professionals, Gail. You didn't cause this."

She nodded, but didn't look convinced. Kotler put a hand on her shoulder.

"Agent Denzel and I will find Aslan and the rest of the people who did this, don't worry."

She shook her head. "I'm not worried about that, really. I'm more worried that now Aslan has my father's stone, as well as the map."

Kotler smiled then. "Well, he has the map at least."

He explained the swap he'd made, replicating the stones before taking them to Van Burren's home. "Wherever Aslan is headed, he'll be disappointed once he gets there. The fake stones won't help him."

"Very clever," Gail said, giving a quick smile. "But he's still got the map."

"So do we," Denzel said, placing a digital tablet on the table in front of her. "This is a reconstruction of the map based on bits and pieces our guys could pull from the security footage. There are some holes. I was hoping you might be able to fill in those gaps, at least with a description."

Gail shook her head. "I've never seen the map before. I wouldn't know what it looks like."

She studied the image on the tablet for a moment, then said, "But this does seem familiar. I think …"

She stood and went into the small office just off of the living area of her apartment.

She returned a moment later with a framed photo. It was a black and white image, taken in Vietnam. A much younger Van Burren was crouched alongside Gail's grandfather, Edward McCarthy, and a few Montagnards mercenaries who were grinning for the camera. At their feet was an old foot-locker turned on its side, allowing hundreds of documents to spill out. Also in the locker was the Atlantis stone, which Kotler recognized immediately, and there, propped against the box, was a half folded map.

"That's it," Kotler said, holding the photo close to his nose, examining the grainy image of the map. "I think that has the bulk of what we're missing from the security footage," he said, looking up and showing Denzel.

The agent leaned in and looked closely. He turned then and asked one of the other agents in the room, "Can you take this photo to IT and have them scan it? See if they can complete the map from the security footage."

The agent nodded and took the photo, frame and all, leaving the room.

Kotler turned back to Gail. "You may have just cracked this with a 40 year old photo."

"I do what I can," Gail smiled. "Now, when do we leave?"

"Leave?" Kotler asked.

"To follow that map," Gail said. "Now that we have it, and we have the *real* stones, we need to go find Atlantis!"

Kotler smiled, but before he could respond Denzel said, "First, we don't know exactly where this map leads just yet. And even once we do, we'll be going there to intercept Aslan and his people. That makes it far too dangerous for you to come along."

Gail gave him a stern look. "Actually, it seems just as dangerous for me here, considering Aslan grabbed me right from my own apartment. So in that case, I'd rather be surrounded by FBI agents. And then there's the fact that one of those stones is my personal property."

Denzel nodded. "That's true, but it's also evidence in this case. You'll get it back when we've resolved all of this."

"That was never my agreement," Gail said. "My grandfather left that stone to me and I gave it to Dr. Kotler for safe keeping. He's the one who gave it to *you*, which means I never gave permission for it to be in FBI custody. You're basically stealing it from me."

Denzel was about to speak up against this when Kotler interrupted. "Roland ..." Denzel shot him a look. "*Agent Denzel*," Kotler corrected. "She does have a point. But beyond that, she might actually be useful in solving this. She knows more about the stone and her grandfather's business than anyone. If Van Burren was using the business as a front for his smuggling operation, having her onboard might be the fastest way to break this open."

Denzel opened his mouth to say something, then promptly closed it again. There was a pause—possibly a counting of ten—and Denzel finally said, "Ms. McCarthy, we could certainly use your assistance in this case. But you'll be acting under my authority while the investigation is ongoing. You'll stay when I tell you to stay, and you'll go when I tell you to go, and that is the final word."

"But I'm going to wherever the map takes us," Gail said, firmly.

Denzel didn't reply, but instead went to find the IT team, and to see if the map was complete yet.

Kotler grinned after his friend, and wondered how much trouble they'd all just agreed to.

PART 2

CHAPTER 11

BATTICALOA, SRI LANKA—FEBRUARY 2, 2017

BATTICALOA WAS NEARLY 70 MILES SOUTH OF Trinconmalee, the more resort-like region of Sri Lanka. Though Batticaloa lacked some of the luxuries of Trinconmalee, it was no less beautiful or intriguing. It had once been the capital city of Sri Lanka, until that honor was moved clear to the other side of the island, to Colombo.

The city was one of the worst hit in the 2004 tsunami, and in many ways the locals were still putting their lives together more than a decade later. Buildings had been repaired, rebuilt, or torn down. Streets had long been cleared. But the marks of the tsunami remained on the lives of the people who lived there. Kotler could see it with every glance toward the pristine beaches, with every strong gust of wind through the palms.

He was seated at an outdoor table at a beachside cafe, only a short walk from the hotel where he, Agent Denzel, and Gail McCarthy were staying. At the moment, the three of them were contemplating the latest set of clues deciphered from the map.

Kotler shook his head as he leaned back, bringing the palms of his hands up to rub at his tired eyes.

The three of them had been moving ceaselessly over the past month, attempting—and failing—to track Aslan, using the map to try to get ahead of him. Their only advantage, as far as Kotler could see, was that they had Kotler's resources and experience in this sort of work and, of course, the presence of Gail McCarthy.

She was quite beautiful, Kotler admitted. And quite intelligent. Both factors he considered frequently, as the two of them worked closely on deciphering the symbols and language of the original map makers, as well as the hand-written notes Edison himself had made. Kotler found himself distracted by her at times, wandering into chitchat about the beauty of Sri Lanka, or the mysterious nature of the stones, or the beguiling possibility of actually finding *Atlantis*.

Luckily he had Denzel, the world's worst wingman, there to keep him on track. All potentially romantic interludes were interrupted before they could really start, usually by a grumbling update from Denzel about the whereabouts of Aslan.

Their beachside conversation, in fact, had turned at some point from the map to Aslan himself.

"It would help if we knew his real name," Denzel groused.

"If we're going to go that far," Kotler said, chuckling, "it would help even more if he'd simply cuff himself and turn himself in."

Denzel gave him a frown, and then stood from the table, stretching. "I'm starting to think we're getting nowhere, and this trip was a bust."

"At least the scenery is enchanting," Gail smiled.

Denzel shook his head. "We're not—"

"—here on a vacation," Kotler and Gail intoned together, both laughing at Denzel's reaction.

"Right," Denzel said. "I'm going to go back to my room to make a few phone calls, see if anyone back home has uncovered anything. You two keep working on the map. It's gotten us this far, but if you can't figure out the last leg we'll have to move on to another approach."

He turned and walked back up the beach, toward the hotel.

"He needs to learn how to relax," Gail said.

Kotler watched after Denzel for a moment, then sunk back into his chair a bit. "He's right, though. It's been over a month since we started chasing Aslan and whatever this map is pointing to, and we haven't made much progress on either front."

"I don't know about Aslan," Gail said. "But I'm excited about how close we are to Atlantis."

Kotler shook his head, then reached forward to grab the cup of coffee he'd been sipping. It was cold now, but he didn't mind. It was more to distract him, to give him something else to focus on for a moment. "You're so certain it's Atlantis," Kotler said. "Why is that? Why did your Grandfather and Van Burren believe that's what they'd found?"

Gail looked at him, and then looked past him to the waves rolling onto the beach, a few feet away. She watched the people strolling by, and Kotler followed her gaze briefly. When she turned back, she said, "I was never all that sure, but I think it may have been Van Burren's suggestion. My grandfather never told me why, at least. He only told me the stories of their travels. Maybe he made up Atlantis, so that it would all seem more exciting to me."

"But you don't think that's the case," Kotler said.

She shook her head, and smiled. "No, I don't. My grandfather wasn't above lying—he did it to protect himself and his family, all the time. I knew that. But he never lied to *me*. Whatever his reasons for thinking the map led to Atlantis, he believed it. So I guess I came to believe it, too."

"And now, here you are," Kotler said, "on a quest taken up by millions over the centuries. And what happens if we find where this map leads, only to discover it's *not* Atlantis after all?"

She laughed, and held her arms wide. "The map has brought us to Sri Lanka—an actual island nation, and one of the places people suspect Atlantis may be found. A country that was almost taken into the sea by a tsunami, just over a decade ago. That can't be coincidence."

Kotler shook his head. "You'd be surprised how deeply coincidence can run," he said. "Don't count it out. But I'll grant you that this does seem to be a likely spot. If we could just solve the last bit of this puzzle, we might actually make it to whatever the map is hiding. And possibly nab Aslan at the same time."

He bent forward again, looking at the large printout they'd brought—the reconstruction of the map, enhanced by NSA imaging technology. There were a couple of gaps, where the photos of the map had been obscured. But those were primarily at the edges, away from the main landmasses and symbols and hand-written notes.

Of course, in those gaps there could be the very key they were missing. The one clue that brought this all together. It frustrated them, and particularly drove Kotler crazy. He was incredibly patient with this sort of work, and frequently had to deal with a lack of a complete picture. But he felt he had an axe to grind with Aslan, and that added more pressure to the situation than what Kotler normally tolerated.

"If only we had this final piece," Kotler said, indicating the gap at the top of the map. "Denzel has had his people scour the security footage for even a millisecond of that part, and so far there's nothing. I just *know* that whatever is there will be the final clue."

Gail leaned forward now as well, and Kotler caught the scent of coconut oil from her skin. Again, she was distracting. But in a way Kotler appreciated greatly, for the moment. Sometimes a good distraction …

He paused, and something clicked in his mind.

"Coconuts," he said.

"What?" Gail looked up at him, puzzled.

Kotler stood and looked toward the rolling Indian Ocean. Near them was a small coconut tree—a nod to one of the island's primary exports. This one had already been harvested for ripe coconuts, but there were a few green bulbs growing toward its top.

"Did you know that Sri Lankan coconuts have been found in ancient cities and ruins as far away as the North-eastern shores of North America? There are dig sites in Canada where thousand-year-old coconuts have been unearthed. They fall into the ocean and are carried by ocean currents to destinations all over the planet."

Gail had stood now and was watching him. The look on her face was a mix of wonder and concern. "What does this have to do with anything?" she asked, but her tone indicated she was as excited as Kotler was. She could sense he was on to something.

"We've been trying to decipher the symbols on that map as a language, and we've had only limited success. But what if some of the information was purely nautical? What if some of those symbols denote currents? Ocean rivers?"

Gail smiled. "That could explain some things," she said. "Do you know enough about that sort of thing to translate it?"

Kotler shook his head but smiled. "No," he said. "But I

don't have to. I happen to know someone who does. And she's local."

CHAPTER 12

EASTERN UNIVERSITY, SRI LANKA

DR. THARUSHI KALLA GREETED THEM AT THE EASTERN University's Oceanic Studies facility. Kotler and Gail had come alone—Denzel was busy responding to queries from the home office, which had the bite of something that had to be dealt with *right now*.

"Besides," Denzel had said, "I don't think I can stomach five more minutes of academic pontification."

"Are you sure?" Kotler asked. "There's sure to be some fascinating data about oceanic currents and tectonic activity in this region."

"That, right there, is justification enough."

Kotler had laughed and let it go, and had driven the rental car to the Eastern University campus. He and Gail were now being given a brief tour of the university's facilities, led by Dr. Kalla herself.

Dr. Kalla was an old friend, though Kotler had never met her in person. He had really only communicated with her by email and Skype, generally seeking out her expertise on oceanic currents and properties as part of his research. This was their first time to meet face-to-face, and she was more than happy to greet them.

"We so rarely get visitors," Kalla said, her Tamil accent making her every word sound intriguing. She was a lovely woman, with the mocha-colored skin of the native population here. Her dark hair was tied back in a fetching pony tail, making her seem more youthful than one would expect from a department head. And yet everything about her demeanor said she was in charge, and quite capable.

Kotler knew that beyond her beauty, she was fiercely intelligent. She had studied at Plymouth University—one of the UK's top universities for Oceanography. And when she'd completed her PhD she had immediately returned to Sri Lanka to teach the brightest minds among her people.

In light of 2004's tsunami, there was a sudden booming interest in Oceanography, and Kalla had been at the forefront of bringing new technology and new resources to her home town university. She was something of a hero here, lauded and respected by her peers, and by the international community as well.

"We're thrilled to get an inside peek at this place," Kotler said, smiling. "And it's so good to meet you in person."

"Yes it is," Kalla beamed. She looked to Gail. "And you as well, Ms. McCarthy. Welcome."

"Thank you," Gail smiled. "We really hope you can help us unlock this map."

Kalla nodded. "It sounds intriguing. Shall we take a look?"

They moved into Dr. Kalla's small office, which was tidy and organized. Her desk was completely free of any objects whatsoever—not so much as an open laptop adorned its surface.

"I often need a large work surface," she explained,

catching Kotler's gaze. "My laptop rests on a slide-out tray, which allows me to access it as needed, and gives me the ability to move it out of the way when I do not."

"You are an anomaly among academics," Kotler smiled. "I didn't believe it was even possible to see the surface of a professor's desk."

Kalla nodded, smiling, and motioned to the desk, where Kotler spread the printed copy of the map they had been studying for over a month now.

It had grown since they'd started. The handwritten notations from Edison were now joined by multi-colored ink notes from Kotler, Gail, and even Denzel—though they were largely limited to what few translations Kotler had managed, along with bits of speculation about certain regions. Sri Lanka was marked on the map, having been one of the few readily identifiable land masses.

Kalla stooped to study the map, and reached into a drawer in her desk to retrieve a large photographer's loupe. She used this to look closer at some of the markings.

"I do not recognize the symbols," Kalla said. "But they do seem to indicate ocean currents, judging by their position and their relation to certain known streams."

"I was hoping that would be the case," Kotler said. "If we can match up this map with some known currents, we might be able to find … what we're looking for."

He had almost said 'Atlantis.' But at this juncture, it didn't seem entirely prudent to mention it. He and Kalla had a mutual respect, but that might fade quickly if she decided he was a loon on a fool's quest.

"I do not recognize these currents, unfortunately," she said. "But that is not surprising."

"It's not?" Gail asked.

Kalla looked up at her and shook her head briefly. "This

region has a great deal of tectonic instability, as I'm sure you are aware. If this map is as old as you say, there is a possibility that the oceanic currents have shifted in the intervening centuries."

Kotler let out a breath. "That's unfortunate. I was hoping you could confirm some of these so we could backtrack to what we're trying to find. But at least we got confirmation that these symbols are actually referring to ocean currents."

"Yes," Kalla said. "And more. These symbols," she indicated a pattern that Kotler had been puzzling over for weeks, "align with some known seamount volcanoes in the Indian Ocean. They are currently inactive, but we believe they erupted more than once over the past three thousand years."

"Seamount?" Gail asked.

Kalla replied, "Forgive me. A seamount is a mountainous structure rising from the seabed, but never quite penetrating the water's surface."

Gail nodded. "So these symbols," she indicated the map, "align with those existing seamounts."

Kalla nodded. "Yes," she said. "I am certain."

"And that is amazing news," Kotler said, awed.

"Why?" Gail asked. "How does it help us?"

"It helps because that makes two points of reference," Kotler said, astonished and smiling. "With our target being the third."

Gail shook her head, and Kotler explained.

"Triangulation," he said. "We know two landmarks now, and their relative distance from each other. So we can use that information to calculate the location and distance of the third."

"Which means we can find it?" Gail asked.

Kotler nodded. "We can find it."

The elation was palpable, and Gail actually squealed a

bit, and then hugged him. Dr. Kalla was smiling as well, but waved off a potential hug. "I am happy to help," she replied.

"I wish we had come to you much sooner," Kotler said, shaking his head. "We've been working on this for over a month."

"Yes, it does seem as if you would have thought to bring an ocean map to an oceanographer a lot sooner," Kalla teased.

Kotler chuckled. "Right. Well, there have been a few mitigating circumstances. But I think this solves a big chunk of our puzzle. Now we just have to work out the exact coordinates of our third location."

Kalla looked back at the map. "I assume this is what you are searching for?" she said, indicating a symbol surrounded by Edison's handwritten notes.

Kotler nodded. "It's a small island, from the look of it. Do you know it?"

"No," Dr. Kalla said. "But despite many popular assumptions, not every small island in the ocean has been mapped. This one could be small enough that no one has paid it much attention."

"It should be at least large enough to support a city," Kotler said. "But it may also be submerged."

If Kalla made the connection between "submerged" and "city," she didn't show it. This was the closest Kotler would ever come to telling her what they were after.

"There is something strange here, however," she said.

"Well, that would be about right. What have you found?" Kotler asked.

"These markings," she indicated a set of lines, swirls, and shapes that ran in patterns around the edge of the map. "They all end at approximately the same latitudes and longitudes. They form a near perfect square."

Kotler, startled, looked closer at the map, and for the first time noticed what Dr. Kalla had spotted. "Damn," Kotler said, stooping and using the photographer's loop to look at the edges of the patterns. "I can't believe I missed that."

"What does it mean?" Gail asked.

Kotler studied the map a bit longer, then said, "It means we need to go talk to Roland."

CHAPTER 13

HOTEL NIRUTHA, BATTICALOA, SRI LANKA

KOTLER LEFT GAIL TO CHAT WITH DR. KALLA, AND tried several times to call Denzel on his satellite phone, with no success. After nearly twenty minutes of this, he retrieved Gail and the two of them took their rental car back to the hotel.

"So what exactly have we just learned?" Gail asked.

"That there was information missing from the map. But also, we happen to have that information with us."

Gail thought about this for a moment. "The stones?"

Kotler nodded, smiling. "And Denzel has those locked away, here in Sri Lanka."

Gail let out a breath. "I can't believe it," she said, her voice nearly a whisper.

Kotler replied, "Me neither. All this time."

Gail smiled at him, and then took out her phone, checking messages and sending texts. "Signal here is terrible," she said.

"Must be," Kotler agreed. "I couldn't raise Roland, even on his sat phone. Could be a problem on my end."

They arrived at Hotel Nirutha nearly an hour later, and made their way to Denzel's room.

They stopped suddenly when they found the door standing open.

Kotler peered inside, holding up a hand to warn Gail back.

The room was a disaster.

Everything had been turned over and torn into. Fluff from the pillows, the mattresses, and the room's sofa was lying in drifts all over the room. The drawers from the dresser had been pulled and turned over.

"What happened here?" Gail asked, quietly.

Kotler shook his head and entered the room cautiously.

Denzel was nowhere to be seen, but that wasn't unexpected. His clothes were scattered among the mess, and as Kotler swept the room with his gaze he saw the sat phone, smashed and lying in pieces near the small desk at the far corner of the room.

Kotler turned and opened the door to the closet. The small room safe had been forced open somehow, and the metal door was twisted and hanging at an obscene angle. The safe itself was empty.

"Someone was here to get the stones," Kotler said.

"They took Roland?" Gail asked, her voice sounding worried.

Kotler turned to her. "We'll need to call local authorities," he said. "But I want you to keep the information about the stones and the map quiet."

Gail nodded.

Kotler picked up the room's phone, but it was also smashed. He used his mobile phone to call the hotel's front desk and tell them to get in touch with the police.

"So they have the stones now," Gail said, despondent.

"No," Kotler replied. "The stones are safe."

Gail gave him a strange look. "But the safe is empty," she said.

"Yes, but they weren't in the safe. Roland had them stored elsewhere."

Gail was hesitant for a moment, a strange expression passing her face, and then she smiled. "So we still have them!" she said.

Kotler nodded. "We still have them. But more important, we need to figure out who has Roland. And I have a feeling I know who that is. I'm just waiting for him to call and confirm."

"Aslan?" Gail asked.

"He told me he had other ways to coerce me. I never thought he meant Roland."

"Do you think he's ok?" Gail asked.

Kotler didn't answer. He wasn't sure that he could.

When the local police arrived, Kotler and Gail both gave their statements. "You'll need to contact the FBI," Kotler told them. "They'll need to be updated on Agent Denzel's situation. They'll send agents here to help with the investigation."

The officers agreed, and after an hour or so of questioning and going back through the information they had, Kotler and Gail were told they could go.

They wandered back to Kotler's room, which was just similar enough to Denzel's that it created a sort of eerie *deja vu*.

The events of the day had been wearying. Kotler sank into one of the plush chairs of his room, and Gail sat on the corner of his bed. "What do we do now?" she asked.

"Unfortunately, I'm out of ideas. The only thing left is to wait."

Gail nodded, and sighed.

In that moment, Gail's mobile phone rang.

She answered, and froze. After a few seconds, she handed the phone to Kotler. "It's him," she whispered.

Kotler felt his blood heat up. He wasn't prone to sudden anger, but Aslan had been pushing his buttons for quite some time now. And this time he'd taken Kotler's friend.

"Aslan," Kotler answered.

"Dr. Kotler, it is just so nice to hear your voice again," Aslan replied. "I hope you're enjoying your stay in Sri Lanka."

"You've abducted a Federal Agent of the United States," Kotler said, his tone bitter and icy. "I don't think you've thought things through on that score."

"It's true, we've put ourselves at great risk," Aslan agreed. "But at this stage of the game, risk is necessary, wouldn't you agree? We're close to finding what we're all after. That's worth having the FBI out looking for me. But I plan to mitigate that risk a bit. You'll help me find the city and retrieve whatever secrets it holds, and I'll let Denzel go. Alive."

The implication was clear. Help, or Denzel dies. Kotler was breathing in even, steady breaths. "If we're really talking about Atlantis here, you're going to need more than my help. If this is a sunken city, it's going to require a skilled dive team."

"Well, that's the best little blessing in all of this, Dr. Kotler," Aslan said. "Unlike you, I have a complete map. And on my map there is a notation. I'm sending it now, along with its translation."

There was a buzz from the phone, indicating a text message. Kotler looked at it, and his eyes widened. He put the phone back to his ear. "You're certain?"

"Could I doubt Mr. Thomas Alva Edison?" Aslan replied.

Kotler fought the urge to roll his eyes and point out that there was only the one Thomas Edison in history books—there was no need to bring his middle name into play. And if this had been a call with a friend or colleague, Kotler would have made that joke.

But Aslan was neither of those things.

"Ok," Kotler said. "I'll help."

"Good!" Aslan said. "I rather thought you might. Oh, and bring Gail McCarthy."

"She stays out of this," Kotler said, clenching his jaw.

"No, sorry," Aslan said with mock sympathy. "I'm afraid I can't allow Ms. McCarthy to go unsupervised. Either both of you show up at the address I'm about to text to you, within the next eight hours, or Agent Denzel will take his last swim in the ocean."

Kotler gripped the phone hard enough that he thought he might crush it with his bare hand. "Fine," he said.

"And the stones," Aslan said. "The real ones. We'll need those as well. I assume you know how to retrieve them?"

"Yes," Kotler replied.

"Good. Now get moving. It will take you nearly all of that eight hours to drive to our location."

And with that Aslan hung up.

Kotler handed the phone back to Gail. She asked no questions, but only nodded. "He has Roland," she said. "And he wants the stones."

"He wants all of us," Kotler said.

CHAPTER 14

THOTUPOLA KANDA, SRI LANKA

Thotupola Kanda, also known as Thotupola Peak, was the third highest mountain in Sri Lanka. It was a six hour drive from their hotel in Batticaloa, and so Aslan had been entirely on the level—they really had needed the entire eight hours.

Retrieving the stones had been simple enough. On their first evening in Sri Lanka, Denzel had stored the case containing the stones in a safety deposit box in a local bank. He had given Kotler one of the two keys, and put him on the signing card. Kotler had been with Gail at the time, puzzling over the map and what little information they'd already deciphered. But Denzel had given Kotler a full run-down of where the stones were and how to retrieve them.

Now the case rested at Gail's feet as they drove through the winding and often ill-kept roads leading into the mountains. Totupola Peak rose before them after the long night's drive, looking majestic in the morning sun.

The address Aslan had given them was off of the main road, on a mostly dirt and shale drive that had seen far better days. It had been cleared recently, as evidenced by several fallen trees and large boulders pushed to the side of the road by something that had large treads, which had left some jarring ruts in the road's surface. It was a bumpy ride, but passable.

They crested a small, tree-covered hill to discover a minor settlement nestled into the mountain.

These were modern buildings, built from steel girders and corrugated siding. There were three small structures set up along a well-tended runway, and at the far end of that was a domed hangar. Out front was a small aircraft—a DHC-6 Twin Otter, Kotler observed.

"Looks like we'll be going for a ride," Kotler said.

"They thought of everything," Gail agreed.

They pulled the rental car to a stop in front of the hangar, and exited the car. No one was in sight at first, and Kotler wondered briefly if they'd come to the wrong place.

Then Aslan exited the door of the hangar.

"Dr. Kotler! So good to see you again," Aslan said, grinning. "And Gail McCarthy. You look so much lovelier without the bag on your head."

"Where is Denzel?" Kotler asked.

"Oh, we'll get to him. Where are the stones?"

Kotler was holding the case, and hefted it by the handle, raising his left hand at the same time, showing that he was unarmed.

Which was the cue for some of Aslan's men to come pouring from the buildings lining the runway. They had automatic rifles leveled at the two of them, and in moments they took the case and patted both Kotler and Gail down, searching for weapons. Others searched the car, using scanning devices to look for trackers or bugs.

"Clear," a man said. His face, like those of the other men, was obscured by a balaclava, and goggles over his eyes.

They had the bearing of ex-military. In fact, Kotler recognized the camouflage patterns on a few of their uniforms. These were ex-US Special Forces—the same branch that Van Burren and McCarthy had belonged to, which raised more questions than it answered.

"Well, I just want to thank you for operating in good faith, Dr. Kotler," Aslan said, smiling. "I really thought you'd try something. Good on you."

"Denzel," Kotler said.

Aslan nodded, and then gave one of his men a look. The man trotted off, rifle in hand, and after a few moments came back with Denzel, hands tied and head covered, stumbling to the spot where everyone was standing.

"Roland, are you ok?" Kotler asked.

Denzel's voice came back muffled and strained, "Never better," he said. "Don't do anything they tell you to do."

"Oh, now Agent Denzel, that would just be a bad idea all around. And besides, Dr. Kotler has *already* given me everything I asked for."

"Then let them go," Denzel said. "You don't need them anymore, so let them go."

"Well, I wouldn't go *that* far," Aslan said, looking up at Kotler and Gail, grinning. "No one knows how to solve an ancient mystery better than our friend Dr. Kotler," he said. "And as for Ms. McCarthy—well, every travel guide tells you to make sure you have good insurance."

"You have enough leverage with just the two of us," Kotler said.

"Leverage is like gold, Dr. Kotler," Aslan said. "You can never have too much."

Aslan nodded to a couple of his men, who immediately stepped forward, taking hold of both Kotler and Gail. They led everyone to the DHC-6.

Kotler knew this plane—it was popular with bush pilots,

especially in Canada. It could take around 20 passengers, with light cargo, and had a range of nearly 800 miles, depending on conditions. Kotler had been in one that went down in the wilderness of Canada, some years earlier. Seeing one here, in the tropics of Sri Lanka, was a bit surreal, but Kotler supposed it would be a fairly good plane for getting around in the region, as long as one didn't need to land on water.

"There's no water landing gear on this plane," Kotler said as they were jostled along.

"No," Aslan said. "Very observant."

"So much for the theory that we're searching for Atlantis, then," Kotler replied.

Aslan laughed. "Don't be so sure," he said. "The world is just filled with surprises."

They were forced aboard the plane, along with five of Aslan's men and Aslan himself. One of the men was the pilot, and he took the controls. The others stationed themselves at intervals along the interior of the plane, which had been modified to haul cargo as well as passengers. There were Pelican cases locked and tied down at intervals, distributing the weight evenly and also creating artificial walls within the plane's interior. Kotler and Denzel were forced to the back of the plane, where they were handcuffed to metal bars in the floor. Gail was kept somewhere toward the front, out of their line of sight.

After the masked guards had ensured they were locked up tight, Denzel and Kotler were alone with Aslan.

He stood over the two of them, smiling, and said, "I hope you'll have a comfortable ride. No drink service on this flight, unfortunately."

He retreated back to the front of the plane.

Kotler and Denzel, miserable, sat in heaps against the wall of the plane.

Kotler shook his head. "There's something that isn't right about this," he said.

Denzel raised his cuffed wrists as high as he was able. "Oh? I hadn't noticed."

"This plane is all wrong," Kotler said. "And so is Aslan."

"What are you picking up from him?" Denzel asked.

Kotler shook his head again. "I'm not entirely sure. There are pieces, and nothing adds up. I'll have to think about it."

"Think fast," Denzel said. "Because I have a feeling we're going to wear out our usefulness soon."

CHAPTER 15

SOMEWHERE OVER THE INDIAN OCEAN

THEY HAD BEEN IN THE AIR FOR QUITE SOME TIME—
Kotler had no way of knowing how long exactly, but he
judged it to be between an hour-and-a-half and two hours.
Long enough to get several hundred miles away. He
suspected the DHC-6 had been modified with a larger fuel
tank, but that might only add three or four hundred miles to
their range. If he factored in that they would need to make a
return trip, and that they had to fly a couple hundred miles
just to leave the island, wherever they were going had to be
300-500 miles off the coast of Sri Lanka. Give or take.

As far as Kotler knew, there were no islands or anything
else in that range.

At least, not on any modern maps.

He and Denzel chatted about possibilities and plans for a
time, but they exhausted everything they had less than
halfway through the trip. They had both come to realize that
their only chance was to wait and see if an opportunity arose
wherever they were headed. With five armed ex-military as
chaperones, not to mention Aslan, they were more or less at

the mercy of events. But something could still come up—if they were paying attention.

The plane tilted slightly to the port side, angling left as the engines changed pitch.

We're circling for a landing, Kotler realized with a shock.

He had studied maps of this region for almost a month now, and knew with certainty that there were no islands marked in the range they would have flown. Which didn't necessarily discount the presence of one. Even in the era of digitally enhanced optics and low-Earth-orbit satellites, there were still parts of the Earth that went unmapped and unnoticed. In fact, thanks to underwater volcanic activity in this region, a new island could literally pop up over night.

Kotler doubted they would be landing on one of these, however.

The plane descended rapidly, making Kotler's ears pop, and within twenty minutes of their initial descent they touched down. Kotler and Roland were jolted and jostled by the landing, but otherwise came out ok.

Two of Aslan's mercenaries came back and removed the cuffs from Kotler and Denzel, then led them roughly past the stacks of cargo and out of the plane's door. They stumbled down the exit ladder and blinked at the bright sky surrounding them.

They were definitely on an island.

Kotler rotated, looking around at the scenery of the place. They were on a cliff-side runway, which looked to have been hand carved from the small, stony hillside that rose above the forest of the island. From here, Kotler could see the entire coastline in 360 degrees.

This place was *small*. It was covered in tree growth, however, which showed it had been here for quite some time. The forest below them was dense enough that Kotler couldn't see the floor of it, and it stretched for 10 miles or so in one direction, before ending at a roiling coastline.

This island was certainly big enough to be the location of Atlantis, by Kotler's estimate. But there was no sign of a city anywhere.

"Move," one of the masked mercenaries said, shoving Kotler ahead of him.

Kotler exchanged glances with Denzel, who gave him a slight nod. *Be alert*, he was saying. *Be on the lookout.*

If they had any chance of overtaking their captors and escaping this, it would come here. Kotler concentrated on memorizing the path they were taking from the DHC-6. It could be their only chance at getting home.

He was also looking around to see where Gail was, but there was no sign of her *or* Aslan.

They were led down a path, which spiraled around the outer edge of the small mountain. It eventually led down to a plateau just above the forest top, where four small, temporary outbuildings had been erected.

Aslan stepped out of one of them. Two of his soldiers had been standing guard in front of it, and they joined him as he walked away.

"Welcome to the island, gentlemen," Aslan said.

"Where's Gail?" Kotler asked.

Aslan smiled. "She's safe, Dr. Kotler As safe as she can be. And she'll stay that way, as long as you and Agent Denzel continue to cooperate."

"I want to see her," Kotler said.

Aslan shook his head, sadly. "I'm afraid I can't allow that, Dr. Kotler. But don't worry. I've taken care of her."

There was a note of something in Aslan's voice, but Kotler had no time to consider it before he and Denzel were shoved ahead, toward one of the out buildings.

They were led inside, where they were greeted by an operations center.

There were numerous folding tables lining the walls, with computers and smart tablets arranged neatly. One wall had a large display mounted to it—presumably a meeting area, judging by the folding chairs arranged around it. These were the only chairs in the room.

In the center of the space was another, larger folding table, this time covered in printouts as well as tablets. And among the various maps and pages was a familiar sight—the Atlantis map. Or Edison map, depending on one's personal preference, Kotler supposed.

Kotler's handcuffs were removed, and he was roughly nudged toward the table. Denzel was kept with his hands bound, and a guard at his elbow.

Kotler examined the items on the table, including a large satellite map that had to represent the island they were currently standing on. Since this island wasn't on any *official* maps, to Kotler's knowledge, that meant these images were coming from a private satellite. Or a commissioned one, at least. Something available for public leasing, perhaps.

Kotler studied the satellite map, and looked up at Aslan.

"You already know where the city is," he said.

Aslan chuckled. "We've known for more than a month. We've been here several times now."

Kotler shook his head. "Then why do you need me? I only just discovered the location yesterday."

"We needed the stones," Aslan said. "And, we needed someone to interpret what they reveal."

Kotler understood now.

Somehow, Aslan and his people had been ahead of them all this time. They'd found the island while Kotler, Gail, and Denzel were still chasing vague leads. While Kotler was still struggling just to *locate* the island, Aslan was busy making plans to abduct the three of them and use them to get what he was after.

Kotler felt like a complete imbecile.

"Don't feel too bad, Dr. Kotler," Aslan said in mock sympathy. "You've done very well, considering you didn't have all of the resources and information you needed. I'm actually impressed with how far you've gotten. Now, let's take it the rest of the way."

Aslan stepped forward, put his hands on the table and leaned toward Kotler. The maps and papers were between them, and the light from above cast Aslan's face into a sinister shadow. "We're close, Kotler," Aslan said, all of his practiced refinement draining away. There was a note of something in his voice—the ecstasy of fanaticism. Whatever Aslan was after, it was *big*. "Help me find it, and I can promise you that you will go free."

"And the others?" Kotler asked.

Aslan stared at him for a moment, a strangely contemplative expression on his face, and then he stood straight again. "It all depends on your cooperation," he said.

Kotler considered this. From his body language, Aslan showed he was tense, ready to pounce. He was excited about this discovery, it was clear. But that tension was masking any sign of duplicity or sincerity in his words. Kotler tried to read through it, to get some hint as to Aslan's plans, but failed.

"I'll help," Kotler said.

Aslan smiled. "I thought you might," he said "And let's not pretend. This isn't *just* about saving your friends. You're curious, aren't you? You want to know ... is Atlantis *real?* And I can answer that for you right now, Dr. Kotler. It is. It's as real as anything you've ever known. And we are going to bring its treasures home."

CHAPTER 16

ATLANTIS ISLAND

Kotler had started referring to this place, mentally, as 'Atlantis Island,' mostly as a point of reference. The satellite map showed him that it was a fairly ancient volcanic island that had cooled possibly a million years earlier, by his estimate. There was no way to know for certain without some geographic exploration and discovery, but at the moment he had only some educated guesses to guide his thinking.

The satellite map was marked with several dots and bits of writing. "Alpha" and "Beta" were two sites close to where they now stood. "Omega" was further in. Kotler guessed these might be parts of the city structure, if it was here.

He had been working with Aslan close to his side for more than an hour now. Denzel was cuffed and being kept in a chair across the room, with two armed guards on either side of him. This was less about keeping Denzel put and more about reminding Kotler of the consequences of non-compliance.

Kotler was complying, though. He wouldn't risk Denzel or Gail being hurt because of him. But, if he was being completely honest with himself, he was also compelled by curiosity. This place was strange, and it held mysteries. And he intended to solve them.

"These areas," Aslan said, pointing out some dots and notes on the satellite image, "are where Van Burren and his people found the largest deposits of artifacts so far. They've stripped them bare. Not so much as a gold-plated penny in any of them."

"So Van Burren has been raiding Atlantis all these years?" Kotler asked.

"Since a few years after the Vietnam conflict," Aslan said. "He and McCarthy spent a small fortune tracking this place down. They looked in hundreds of place before coming here. Van Burren was the one who actually solved the problem of the map's currents. He was smarter than people credited him for being."

Kotler caught a strange note in Aslan's voice—almost nostalgic. Did he *care* for Van Burren? And if so, why would he have had the man killed?

"I don't understand," Kotler said. "If Van Burren knew where this island was all along, and you knew that about him, what am I doing here again? What riddle do you need me to solve, Aslan?"

He put a finger on the ancient map, and traced the light square formed by the original symbols and notations. He then nodded to one of his men, who brought the two stones forward and placed them on the table in front of the two men.

"We know some of the history of this place," Aslan said "We know one of the secrets of Atlantis."

Kotler felt a thrill, in spite of himself. After all, he was standing on an island that held an ancient secret—one that had titilated and tantalized millions of would-be and real explorers for centuries. Any new information about Atlantis would be exciting, and Kotler just couldn't help his interest.

"What Plato recorded in *Timaeus* and *Critias* was the destruction of Atlantis, for sure. But he was interpreting things through a narrow focus. He was seeing an event he had never encountered before, and couldn't explain. Something our friends in Sri Lanka would readily relate to."

Kotler thought for only an instant, and said, "A tsunami."

Aslan smiled. "A tsunami," he agreed. "This entire region has a great deal of tectonic activity. And what we know now is that a few thousand years ago there was an earthquake near Sumatra, just as there was in 2004. And that earthquake triggered a wave that grew exponentially over thousands of miles, until it reached this island. And washed over it."

Kotler shook his head. "The destruction must have been incredible," he said. He thought for a moment. "There's no way Plato saw this first hand. But there has long been speculation that he heard the story from someone else, and turned it into something apocryphal and allegorical. He used it as a framework to warn his people of the dangers of avarice and greed."

"That's what my …" Aslan started, then paused, took a breath, and said, "That's right. That's what we believe happened."

Kotler didn't bother asking who the 'we' was in Aslan's mind. He knew he wasn't likely to get an answer.

"So a tsunami comes in and wipes out Atlantis, leaving very few survivors. Those who *do* survive go on to tell their story elsewhere, and eventually they blend into native cultures in this part of the world. Their own culture vanishes overnight. And all that's left are stories. Oh, and a map with a couple of stone artifacts."

"Exactly," Aslan said, grinning. "We believe a priest or some other official was one of the survivors. He took the stones with him. The map may have been made after the fact. There's really no way to know for sure. But the stones were meant to be keys to something much bigger than any treasure Van Burren and McCarthy pillaged over the years. *Much bigger.*"

"At some point the waters receded and the remains of the city stayed behind," Kotler said. "Untouched, until .. what? Thomas Edison found them?"

"That's the story," Aslan said, nodding and smiling. "Van Burren tracked down some of Edison's papers, and along with the map he recovered in Laos they had enough information to start looking. He more or less got lucky on finding the island itself. He didn't have *you* to help. But I do. And now you're going to get me into that hidden chamber."

"But first we have to find it," Kotler said.

Aslan nudged the stones toward Kotler.

Kotler sighed, glanced across the room at Denzel, who was bound and not happy about it. He then picked up the stones and clicked them together, forming an ornate square.

He placed this on the map, studied it for a moment, and then turned it. He studied a few more minutes, and turned it again.

It took a few tries, but eventually he felt he had it aligned properly.

"There," he said, sitting back.

Aslan bent and peered at it. "What do you see?"

"A square rock sitting on a piece of paper," Kotler said. "We're one pair of scissors short a full set."

Aslan chuckled. "Funny," he said. "Now, what do you *really* see, before I have one of my men remove Agent Denzel's eyes."

Kotler took a deep breath and let it out in a rush. He stepped forward again, and started examining the stone and the map as a whole.

The patterns of the map did align perfectly with the markings on the stone. But that was as much as Kotler knew, for the moment. He'd had very little success translating the symbols on either map or stone over the past month. And that may have, in part, been due to having an incomplete picture. But looking at the items together, for the first time, did little to make a translation jump out at him.

He studied the contours of the stone. There were lines and symbols bending over the curved edges, joining their mates on the map itself. Whoever had created these had been a master craftsman, and had taken the contours of the stone into account. It was as if someone had placed a large, clear drop of water on the map, magnifying the surface, giving it a three-dimensional feel.

"Oh you clever, clever map maker" Kotler whispered.

"You have something?" Aslan said, leaning in closer, losing his menacing air in light of possible discovery.

Kotler grinned and straightened, as did Aslan. "There are two maps," Kotler said. "Whoever made this created one map, which shows the location of the island itself. And, with the advent of the stones, he crafted a *second* map, of the *island*. Look here," Kotler pointed now at a marking on the stones, toward one edge. "That symbol indicates the mountain." He pointed now at the satellite map that Aslan's people had laid out on the table. His finger landed on the Alpha site. "This is one of the locations you say Van Burren raided?"

Aslan nodded. "Picked clean."

Kotler now pointed back to the stone, and another symbol. "This symbol lines up with that. And this one lines up with Beta. And this one Omega. And there are three other sites besides, though ..." Kotler paused, peering at the symbols, and then at the satellite map. "Those are gone," he said.

"Gone?" Aslan asked.

"Under water," Kotler said. "They'll take a dive team to explore them. They're pretty far from the shoreline, judging by the satellite imagery. This island used to be much bigger."

Aslan nodded, thinking. "Ok. I can arrange for dive teams. But the Omega site—that's a much bigger location. A proper city," he said. "And there is a chamber in there somewhere."

"How do you know this, exactly?" Kotler asked.

Aslan laughed. "Edison," he said. "He wrote about it in one of his journals. Part of his dark estate."

"You have the journal?" Kotler asked.

"I have the page," Aslan said. He signaled one of his men, and soon a small rectangular case was retrieved and placed on the table in front of them. Aslan opened it to reveal an old and stained journal page with notes written in pencil. The page was kept between two sheets of glass, preserved. "Edison's handwriting," Aslan said. "We had it verified."

Kotler leaned in and read the page. It was an incomplete entry, but one sentence in particular jumped out at him.

We have located a hidden chamber, deep within the main city, and have thus far been unable to open the great door.

"Where is the rest of the journal?" Kotler asked.

Aslan shook his head. "Doesn't exist. Not anymore. It was destroyed in a fire, and only a few pages were saved. This is the only page that contains anything regarding Atlantis."

"This isn't much to go on," Kotler said.

"It's gotten all of us here so far," Aslan smiled.

Kotler couldn't fault that statement, and so he concentrated instead on studying the map and stone once more. He focused on the Omega site now, looking for any clue as to the location of a chamber. After several minutes he stood straight again, rubbing his eyes. "There's nothing here that I can identify as a hidden chamber," he said.

Aslan studied him for a long, silent moment, then

nodded. He looked up at the two men standing beside Denzel, who was slumped miserably in the chair. "Kill him," Aslan said.

"Wait!" Kotler cried, rushing forward only to be held at bay when one of the men turned and aimed a rifle at his chest. Kotler held up his hands. "All I'm saying is that there's nothing on the stone or map to indicate the chamber! We need to *go there*. And in that, Agent Denzel will be useful in helping me solve this."

"You're just trying to save your friend," Aslan said.

"Yes," Kotler agreed. "And it's also true. I need help, and I doubt you and your men will want to slog around with me in the ruins of an ancient sewer system or whatever else we might find there."

Aslan laughed then, and it was a sharp, loud sound. "Well, that's imaginative, Dr. Kotler." He thought for a moment, then said, "Alright. Agent Denzel can live, as long as he's useful. I might need sudden leverage anyway."

Denzel had sat through all of this as silent as a stone, but at this last bit he laughed and said, "Well, I'm glad I could be your source of *leverage*."

He made a quick glance at Kotler, as if sending him a signal.

Kotler saw the look, heard Denzel's words, and made a connection he was ashamed he hadn't made before. He had allowed himself to be blinded by all of this, and had missed something obvious.

For now, however, there was nothing he could do about that. As long as Aslan had Denzel and Kotler at gunpoint, they were both conscripted into the search for the lost treasure of Atlantis.

And now it was time to enter the city.

CHAPTER 17

THE CITY OF ATLANTIS

THE LONG SLOG THROUGH THE THICK TREES AND underbrush was exhausting, and it took several hours to get from the mountainside base camp to a cleared path, which opened up to reveal a series of stone structures in the distance.

"This was a road," Kotler said, examining the ground beneath their feet. Though it was covered in forest loam and growth, Kotler could still spot a few paver stones here and there. The road had held up well for having borne thousands of years of neglect, including at least one known tsunami. Kotler was reminded of something one of his professors had once told him.

"A civilization is only as good as its roads."

In this case, Atlantis was already showing signs of having been a remarkable civilization indeed.

After a brief respite they trudged on, and Kotler was grateful that the ancient road meant their journey was a bit easier, at least.

Kotler and Denzel were being escorted by two different mercenaries this time. Along with Aslan, they were a party of five, with one armed man leading and one bringing up the rear. Both were highly alert, and both held their automatic rifles at the ready.

Kotler and Denzel had fallen into a rhythm beside each other, with Aslan a few steps ahead. There was no real chance to actually *talk* to each other, unfortunately. No way to discuss what they'd both concluded, and no way to plan against their captors. Not openly.

But Kotler saw that Denzel was watching. He was taking in everything, looking for opportunities, assessing the odds.

Kotler did the same, examining their surroundings for some place that might give them shelter or a tactical advantage. He eyed the two armed men, wondering if he had the strength to take one of their weapons. He somehow doubted it—these were trained soldiers who were fresh for the fight. They could easily slog ten miles through tropical forest, with fully loaded packs, and still take men down with their bare hands. Kotler and Denzel both had combat and hand-to-hand training, but that didn't even the odds much.

And so, hours after their journey started, they finally crested a small rise and saw the city sprawled out in front of them, almost close enough to touch.

Within the next half hour they were walking through an ancient stone archway, where a large door must once have stood, and into the inner streets of the city.

Kotler had been silent before, but here he fell into an absolute stunned daze.

All around him was a city made of precisely cut and placed stones, many of which were so large they would have been impossible for one or even two men to lift by hand. And yet everywhere Kotler looked, he saw exacting architecture. The stones of the walls, the streets, even the archways were so tightly seamed that even after thousands of years nothing had managed to grow in or through them. Here, in a fertile tropical environment, there were no vines. No sprouted saplings. No grasses or mosses.

In some ways it looked as if the city had been active and busy only seconds before Kotler and the others had entered.

The preservation wasn't total, of course. As they rounded corners they came to areas where walls had toppled into the streets, roofs had collapsed on some of the buildings, and nature had won the day after all, managing to plant itself in a small pocket of the place, though appearing to be somehow aware that it could venture no further than these crumbling, claimed footholds.

Kotler felt the overpowering thrill he always felt when discovering something ancient and marvelous. He'd felt this way a number of times in his life, in fact, while exploring tombs and lost cities and ancient sites. He had felt this way when he'd first set foot in the Viking 'City of Gold' in Pueblo. It was a sensation he never grew tired of.

And yet, once again, he was feeling it while at gunpoint, or otherwise under threat of death. Maybe the two simply had to go hand in hand.

"It's incredible," Kotler said.

"Yes," Aslan agreed. "Now, find me my hidden chamber, Dr. Kotler, or this will be your tomb."

Kotler looked at Aslan, his expression pained. "You've literally been waiting this entire trip to say that."

Aslan bristled a bit, for once, and said, "I have not." But his body language said otherwise.

They kept on through the city, and Kotler took out a smart tablet that contained photos of the map, the stones, and the satellite imagery. He compared them with what he was seeing now. "Well, there's no map to the city itself," He said. "At least not from what I've been able to interpret. But there are symbols on the stones that align with some of what I'm seeing here." He indicated some markings on one of the walls, at the corner of two streets. They were carved glyphs. "Street signs," Kotler said. "Markers left so people could navigate the city. Probably here for guests."

"Like us," Aslan said. "Now, where do they say to go?"

"This way," Kotler replied.

They pushed on through the maze of ancient city streets and buildings. Again Kotler was struck by how well *preserved* everything was. There were no artifacts to speak of, though there was some debris here and there. A thorough search could potentially turn up a treasure trove of cultural finds, and Kotler was already considering how he could get a team here "once this is all over."

Assuming he and Denzel survived, of course.

They came to a long passage, with stone walls that rose high into the air on either side of them. This was the final symbol from the 'street map' portion of the stones, as far as Kotler could tell. And from the looks of it, this was an entrance to something sacred to the Atlantean people. A temple, perhaps.

"I think this is the place," Kotler said, eyeing the passage.

At its far end was a large building that remained impossibly high and untouched. It rose above the surrounding walls, and was as ornate as any European church Kotler had ever seen. The street they were on rose to meet it, as if it were built on a higher foundation than the rest of the city.

To their right, Kotler spotted something on the wall, and leaned in to inspect it closer.

"Paint," Kotler said.

Aslan leaned in as well. "Paint? The people of Atlantis used paint on their walls?"

Kotler shook his head. "No," he said. "This is too modern. Though not *that* modern. It looks like … it seems to be some kind of survey marker. Old. I can't really say for sure, but I'm guessing this was left here by Van Burren's team. Or possibly before that."

"Edison," Aslan said, his voice awed. "This could have been left by Edison."

"Maybe," Kotler replied. "Without testing the paint I have no idea. But I think it was left as a marker for others to find. A sign to say this is it."

"This is it," Aslan echoed. After a quiet moment he clapped his hands together, sending a sharp crack echoing against the stone walls of the street. "Well then, let us waste no further time. Shall we?"

"We'll need to proceed with caution," Kotler said. "We have no idea what lies beyond this point, and we're about to enter a sacred site, by all indications. It could be protected."

"It could be a church," Aslan said. "And one that my ... one that people have entered before. Van Burren and his men. Edison and his. We will follow their path, and we'll be fine."

Kotler nodded, and stepped in behind the front guard again, alongside Denzel. Aslan, this time, brought up the rear with the second guard. He may have been all bravado and gung-ho to charge into the ancient structure, but he was perfectly willing to let others take the risk of entering *first*.

As they mounted the steep slope of the cobbled streets, the passage began to close in around them. They passed under an arch that took them from the open-air streets of the city and into a tunnel, lit by sunlight from large, angled shafts. As they got deeper in, they each took out electric lanterns that lit the stone around them in flickering waves of shadow and white light. Kotler spotted several mounts for torches on the walls, and at one point he was able to see the arching ceiling, covered in ancient soot that he *yearned* to sample and carbon date.

Another time.

After some distance the passage became level and flat, and opened into a slightly larger chamber that ended abruptly at a large, iron door.

The door was framed in a stone arch in the wall of the place, and was dotted with hundreds of riveted knots of iron, forming a gridwork from top to bottom. Within this grid-work were intricately carved stone tiles—their patterns faint with millennia of dust and, from what Kotler could deter-mine, worn by thousands of reverent caresses.

Long ago—long before Edison or anyone else has redis-covered this place—this door had been the thin barrier between the people of Atlantis and some holy treasure within. And many thousands of people had come here and touched these stones as a prayer. That was how Kotler saw this place, and he knew instinctively that he was right.

He stared at the door for a moment, feeling a sickening twist of emotions. He was truly enthralled by this place, and all the hopeful secrets it had to offer. If this was, indeed, the true Atlantis—the legendary city that Plato described, swal-lowed by the ocean, perhaps as payment for the hubris of its people—it was a place of immense historic value. But more than that, it was a testament to the innovative soul of humanity. Kotler looked at the tight seams of stone in the walls and the streets. He looked at the immense wood and iron door standing in front of him, still a solid barrier after *millennia*. Here Kotler could see one of the high points of humanity's genius. It was thrilling. It was inspiring.

And then came the realization that he was aiding in sacking it. He was working for someone who wanted the treasures of this place, not out of historic interest or with any sense of reverence or respect, but for the sole purpose of greed and avarice. He was helping evil to take a foothold here, to exploit what this great city represented, for nothing more than personal gain.

Plato's creed about the hubris of man was playing out thousands of years after his works first appeared, and it made Kotler want to vomit.

Two large, iron rings were mounted at head-height in the great door. Aslan stepped forward now and examined these, glancing back over his shoulder. "Door handles?" he asked.

Kotler shook himself out of the trance of his thoughts, looking closer at the large rings in the door. The best way to deal with this was to solve the mystery of this place while continuing to look for opportunities to escape. So for now, the door was what required Kotler's attention.

"Only one way to find out," he said, nodding toward the door, an invitation for Aslan to give the handles a try.

Aslan grinned. "Oh, I don't think I'll be testing these," he said. "You could be right, after all. This could be a trap. I think we'd better have someone more *expendable* give them a go."

He looked at Denzel, who sighed and held up his cuffed wrists.

Aslan nodded to one of the guards, and they removed the cuffs, then shoved Denzel toward the door.

Kotler joined him, staring at the two rings and the stone tiles adorning the iron surface.

"I'm about to have a bunch of poison darts shot into me, aren't I?" Denzel asked.

Kotler smiled. "I doubt it. After all this time, any poison would likely have faded in potency anyway. It's more likely that a large boulder will come crashing into you, smooshing you into paste."

"You have always been a comforting presence in my life, Kotler," Denzel said.

"I don't think there's anything to worry about," Kotler replied. "This was a place of reverence and worship. I think any traps that might be here are going to be *inside*. They may be triggered by the door opening, but that's something we'll have to deal with as we come to it."

Denzel nodded.

"Dr. Kotler," Aslan said, "You'll be over here with us. I can't risk anything happening to *you*."

"This guy is a peach," Denzel said as Kotler stepped back, keeping his eyes on his friend.

Denzel stood now in front of the door, and rolled his head from side to side, clearing any cricks or tension. Kotler watched him go through this relaxation routine, and silently prayed that his friend would be safe.

Denzel reached up and took each of the iron rings in a hand, braced himself, and *pulled*.

Nothing happened.

He pulled again, harder, grunting with the effort, and again nothing happened.

"Twist them," Kotler said, making little twisting motions with his hands, smiling in encouragement.

Denzel gave him a sour look, but did as he was told, attempting to twist the rings before pulling them.

They did move. That much, at least, was encouraging. As Denzel struggled to turn them, they turned very slightly, clicking against something inside the door.

That was when Kotler realized what needed to be done.

"Wait," he said, stepping forward.

The two guards raised their weapons.

"Oh for God's sake," Kotler said. "Can we give the guns a rest? Where am I going to go? Look, I just realized that we're skipping a step here." He turned to Aslan. "I need the stones."

Aslan studied him for a moment, then shrugged off the pack, shuffled through its contents, and removed the two stones, which were currently fitted together and wrapped in a cloth. He handed the square assemblage to Kotler.

THE ATLANTIS RIDDLE 163

Kotler turned and walked back to the door, stepping in beside Denzel. He looked at the stones, and then at the door. He turned the stones several times, holding them up, examining the patterns next to those of the stone tiles on the door's surface. When he found a match, he lifted the square to the door, and pressed it against the surface in a specific spot.

There was a clacking sound from within the door.

Everyone froze.

Kotler grinned, and took up one of the two rings, nodding for Denzel to take the other.

"Wait!" Aslan said.

"It's fine," Kotler said. "There won't be any trap."

"How do you know?" Denzel asked.

"Because we have the key," Kotler said, nodding to the stones. "On three?"

Denzel nodded, and Kotler counted up. When he said 'three,' the two of them turned and pulled the rings.

More clacking from within, and this time the door pulled free of the wall with a loud and echoing metal-on-metal screech that set Kotler's teeth on edge, but also made him want to laugh out loud.

The door tilted away from them, receding into the wall, and then lay flat upon the ground. It was thick, almost by a foot, and it made for a slight stair step up into a darkened tunnel beyond the wall. On either side of the door were chains that ran up and into the darkness, presumably linking it to something within the structure. Activating something, Kotler was sure, though he kept that information to himself.

They had done it.

They were in.

"Very good, gentlemen," Aslan said. "Now, let's go find the treasure of Atlantis!"

CHAPTER 18

TEMPLE OF ATLANTIS

INSIDE THE STRUCTURE IT WAS DAMP AND DANK. A musty aroma wafted up from the downward sloping tunnel that stretched before them. This space had not seen a human presence in a very long time.

They used the lanterns to provide light, and as they descended the corridor eventually opened up into a larger space. From what Kotler could tell, the space was a perfect circle—a spiraling pattern of precisely cut stones formed its floor, and in the very center was a dais and podium. They made their way to it.

"This was a gathering hall," Kotler mused aloud. "Maybe some sort of ceremonial space. Kind of austere," he observed. "It's surprising."

"Why surprising?" Aslan asked.

"Because you would expect there to be artifacts here. Ceremonial devices. Bits of cloth from banners, or bits of shaped iron or wood. This culture clearly had access to iron, which is almost unfathomable. It must have been unbeliev- ably valuable, considering it had to have been imported. And we already know they had a penchant for gold, otherwise

Van Burren wouldn't have bothered with the place. I'm starting to realize that whoever built all of this didn't originate here. They must have come from the mainland, discovered this place, and turned it into a fortress."

"And why would they go to that much trouble?" Aslan asked.

Kotler shrugged. "Plato described this society as being arrogant and greedy. Maybe they were trying to protect their treasure by keeping all of it away from anyone who might have the strength to take it. You have to admit, the Indian Ocean is one hell of a moat. They could easily defend this place from even some of the largest navies in history, given that they had iron for weapons and fortifications, and a significantly advanced knowledge of architecture. This place has withstood thousands of years of natural siege—it would stand up to anything that the people of Plato's era could have thrown at it."

"Fascinating," Aslan said. So what does it mean that there is nothing here?"

Kotler wasn't sure how to answer that, because he frankly didn't know. He shrugged and offered, "We know nothing about Atlantean culture, if that's truly who built this place. Maybe they were extremely conservative."

This seemed to be enough for Aslan, but Kotler knew deep down that it was wrong. He had studied numerous historical cultures, up close, and sacred spaces were almost always adorned with the richest bounty the culture had to offer. The fact that this place stood empty meant it had been cleared at some point. Perhaps the Atlanteans had managed to rescue their most treasured cultural artifacts before the tsunami claimed the island.

If that was the case, Kotler knew, then he and Denzel were in a great deal of trouble. More than they had already found themselves in. Because it meant that there was no treasure to find here, and their usefulness would come to an abrupt end as soon as that fact was revealed.

Denzel must have sensed this possibility as well. Kotler watched him for a moment, noticing that he was taking in every square inch of the place, though not as a tourist. He was looking for advantages. Weapons, or escape routes, or anything that might allow them to survive.

Kotler noted that they had not placed him back in cuffs, and Roland had his hands positioned in such a way as to bluff them, to dissuade them from realizing his hands were still free. It could be just the advantage they needed, later.

They came to the dais in the center of the room, and Kotler stepped up, cautiously. He had seen this sort of thing before, and occasionally had discovered, too late, that there were traps in place. One incident in particular, in the Brass Hall he had personally unearthed in Egypt, came to mind. But he suspected that sort of trap wouldn't be the case here. There was nothing to protect, after all.

He examined the podium, which covered in carved symbols across its top, as if a permanent scroll had been opened there. A prompt for whoever administered ceremonies in this place, perhaps.

"Can you translate it?" Aslan asked.

"No," Kotler said, shaking his head. "Do we have a camera? A mobile phone? Can we take a photo of this, so I can work on it later?"

Aslan took out his mobile phone and shot several images, using the lantern to light the podium. He slid the phone back into his pocket without even glancing at Kotler.

A bad sign.

It was clear that Kotler and Denzel were quickly burning through their usefulness. If they didn't find a solution soon, they were going to be gunned down right here in this temple.

Kotler looked around the large space, and spotted a

slender bit of hope. "There," he said, pointing. "That ingress."

They moved toward the arched entryway, which led to a series of switchbacks—a maze like path bending around several stone walls, eventually opening up into a large antechamber. The room beyond was protected by yet another door.

Aslan stepped forward, and Kotler could see a tremble of excitement in him. He reached out and touched the large door, which as it turned out was engraved with the same gold-laced symbols as the stones. Beside the door was a square indention, with tendrils of symbols and shapes spreading from it like a web.

Aslan looked at Kotler, "The key?"

"It's all we have," Kotler said. "We should try it. And this is encouraging," he said, nodding to the door. "This would be the chamber where a culture like this might store treasures and artifacts. This could be it."

Aslan was nearly vibrating with his excitement, and he shucked the backpack to remove the stones again, handing them back to Kotler.

Kotler stepped forward and examined the indention in the wall.

It formed a square that was roughly the same dimensions as the combined stones. Along each side was a series of symbols, forming a pattern that Kotler realized could connect to the patterns on the stones. As he examined them, with the stone held up for reference, he realized that there were numerous points where the patterns of the stones might align with the patterns of the wall.

"At least we get four tries," Roland said.

Kotler shook his head. "I don't think so. Remember these stones contain a series of magnets arranged in a specific pattern. Each magnet has two states—its north and south poles. If you bring two opposite poles into proximity, they'll attract each other, and like poles will repel. That means that there's a specific combination to this lock, and I suspect that if we get it wrong just once, we're screwed."

"So do not get it wrong," Aslan said.

Kotler nodded and again studied the wall and the lock.

This was a bit trickier than the lock outside of the temple. There, Kotler saw immediately that all he had to do was complete the pattern. One touch and the door was unlocked.

But from what he was seeing here, completing the pattern once wouldn't be enough. There were four patterns, and each one could be the right answer.

Which meant, Kotler realized, that they were *all* the right answer.

"It's a combination lock," Kotler said.

"What?" Aslan asked. "Are you joking?"

"No, not at all. See these markings? I think they're digits. To open this we have to find the right sequence. It looks like four different patterns. I can identify all four, but I don't know the sequence for placing them."

Aslan nodded to one of the armed men, who instantly stepped up and raised his rifle. "Figure it out," Aslan said.

"Added pressure isn't exactly going to help," Kotler said.

"First we'll kill Agent Denzel," Aslan said. "Then you. And before you say that would be counter productive, I will return here with explosives if I have to."

"You'd risk bringing this entire temple down on you," Kotler said.

"From afar, yes," Aslan said. "If I have to sift through rubble to get my hands on this treasure, I'm willing to do that."

Kotler studied Aslan's face and knew he wasn't bluffing. He shook his head. The ignorance of this man—the treasures here might be more than simply *gold*. There were secrets in this place—this was a clever culture, filled with brilliant minds. Destroying this temple just to get to the gold inside was like slaughtering the goose to get the golden eggs. It could produce so much *more* than just gold!

But Aslan had the fervor of a man overcome by his desires and his passions.

Actually, it was more than that. Aslan was being *driven*, by something or someone outside of himself. He wanted the treasure, that was certain. But he was also being *compelled*. And somehow, here in the isolation of this city, he'd gotten some sort of signal that whoever was holding his strings was growing weary and impatient. That was why Aslan suddenly had to put pressure on the situation. He'd somehow been pressured himself.

Kotler wondered about this for only a second, and then turned back to the task at hand. "Ok," he said. "Give me just a bit of time and I'll solve this, so that we don't have to ruin a world-changing archeological find."

"You have ten minutes," Aslan said, pointedly setting his watch.

Kotler turned back to the wall and frantically studied the symbols. He held the stones up, aligning them without touching them to the wall's surface, practicing the patterns and trying to see what the combination could possibly be.

He couldn't risk trial and error. With the magnets inside the stones aligned to a specific pattern, and with each point of that pattern having potentially two states, combined with the four positions marked on the wall, there were *millions* of possible combinations. His odds of picking the right combination by chance were impossibly low. And a wrong move could trigger disastrous results for all of them.

As he moved the stones around virtually, something nagged at him. He had seen this before, somehow. It didn't look particularly familiar to him, but he had definitely seen something that related to this.

"The map," Kotler said. He turned to Aslan. "Do you have it?"

"The Edison map? No. But I have photos of it." Aslan produced his phone again, swiped a few times, and handed the phone to Kotler.

Kotler zoomed in on a particular set of handwritten notes. Edison's own handwriting, presenting an odd little sequence that Kotler had taken as some sort of napkin-calculation.

"This is it," he said, studying the sequence, memorizing it.

Aslan looked over his shoulder. "I don't see what you mean," he said. "I don't even see any symbols."

"Not symbols," Kotler said. "A sequence. Edison assigned a number to each side of the stone square. I think he figured out this sequence."

"Perfect," Aslan said. "Open it."

"I have the sequence, but I still have to decipher which side Edison assigned to which number."

Aslan made a frustrated groan and said loudly, "*Open the damned door!*"

Kotler nodded. "There's still time. Let me work on it."

He turned back to Aslan's phone and studied the notations from Edison. There was nothing in the set that would indicate which numbers in the sequence were assigned to which quadrant of the stone.

But maybe Kotler was looking too closely.

He expanded the view and was now looking at the entire map. Now that he knew the square was there—a patch of the map that wasn't covered by symbols matching the stone—he couldn't *avoid* seeing it. Much like those visual puzzles, where a picture of a sailboat actually contains an invisible image of something else, once the hidden image was seen it was hard to *unsee* it.

Thankfully, that helped.

Kotler had studied this map for some time now, but like any puzzle, certain pieces didn't make sense until you put together some other part of the puzzle. Now that he knew that the map and the stone were meant to work together, a vital piece of the puzzle had been solved, freeing him up to notice other details.

There were numbers, written in pencil, dead center of each quadrant of the map. Kotler had assumed they were notations meant to help in a search grid, but now he knew the truth. They were a key.

He looked at the stone square again, this time orienting it to how it would be placed on the map. Once done, he instantly saw that the top was 1, the right 2, bottom 3, and left 4.

He had it.

He slipped the phone into his pocket as he raced back to the wall, and oriented the stone to the first number in the sequence. He placed it in the wall and heard a loud *click*.

He reoriented for the second number, and received another click. Then a third. And before the fourth he took a deep breath and let it out slowly, then placed the stone against the indentation.

Another click, followed by a series of clattering noises from somewhere in the temple. And as they watched, the great door slid upward, opening a passage between the antechamber and the great chamber beyond.

Kotler stood back, stone in hand, and looked into the yawning, darkened opening, then back to Aslan and the others.

"Gentlemen," he said "we're in."

They entered the chamber slowly and cautiously. Denzel

and Kotler were in the lead, of course, followed closely by the first armed guard, then Aslan and the second guard. The passage was just wide enough that two people could walk astride, and as Denzel and Kotler moved into the darkness Denzel held a lantern aloft to light their way.

Kotler concentrated on looking for traps.

The rest of the sanctuary may have been unlikely to have traps or other dangers, but this was the inner sanctum, and the rules tended to change. There was every possibility that this space was protected by everything the Atlanteans could come up with. And given their reputation for cleverness, that could be an awful lot of inventive ways to die.

But as Kotler examined their path, he discovered a few curiosities.

There were definitely indications of traps along the corridor—stones that were at a different level than the rest of the floor, portals in the walls at irregular intervals, narrow shafts that concealed something shrouded in their deep shadows. But the uneven stones were depressed, instead of raised, as if those traps had long since been tripped. The portals and shafts in the walls seemed dormant, and as Kotler had Denzel bring the lanterns closer he saw that there were not threatening daggers or arrows, no darts or spikes to lance out at them.

A new fact was becoming clear to Kotler—and it put him on edge. Their time was running short.

"Do we have any sort of plan yet?" Kotler whispered to Denzel.

"Not a good one," Denzel replied quietly.

"We'll have to go with a bad one, then. And soon."

"That bad?" Denzel asked.

Kotler hefted the key stones, which Aslan had forgotten to retrieve. They weren't particularly heavy, but they might do in a pinch. "Pretty bad," Kotler said. "Wait for the best moment, and do whatever you're going to do. I'll back you."

They moved on through the passage, with Kotler still checking for traps along the path, and finally they came to a grand opening.

It was a large, cylinder-shaped room that rose high above them. Along the walls were stacks of rotting wooden shelves, some hanging high up along the shaft of the room, accessible, Kotler guessed, only by ladder. There were also ornate tables, still in surprisingly good shape, placed strategically around the room. On one of these rested an object that wasn't readily identifiable. Kotler moved toward that table, even as Denzel settled back a bit, hanging close to the room's only obvious exit.

"What is that?" Aslan asked.

"No idea," Kotler said, though as he reached the table where it rested, he saw that it was an old leather journal, possibly only a hundred or so years old. He picked it up gingerly, examining it, and shook his head in disbelief. "This belonged to Thomas Edison," he said.

He looked up to see Aslan, standing close, with a disgusted expression on his face. One of the two guards stood to his right, weapon held casually but deliberately.

"It's gone, isn't it?" Aslan asked. "All of it. Edison got to it first. We've been chasing a ghost."

Kotler studied him. The abject disappointment wasn't all that unexpected, but there was something else underlying it. Some hope dashed that had been a driving force for Aslan all along. And more. Kotler could see that Aslan was holding a pose that read 'shame' as clear as day. He had let someone down, Kotler deduced. Someone he cared about was going to be very disappointed in him. Even after all of this.

Their time was ticking down in seconds now, Kotler realized.

Denzel, apparently, realized it, too.

In a sudden burst, Denzel leapt at the guard nearest him. The man shouted a warning, and managed to squeeze off a few quick rounds from the automatic before Denzel had him tackled and disarmed. Without hesitation, Denzel fired, killing the man. There could be no dealing with prisoners under these circumstances—this was war.

Kotler leapt forward then, but focused on Aslan. The smaller man was closer, for starters, but also less of a challenge to subdue. And as he was the one in charge, the second guard wouldn't risk shooting him to get to Kotler.

At least, that was the theory.

As Kotler pulled Aslan along with him, the mercenary took aim and started firing. It was only by luck that Kotler tripped just at that moment, bringing Aslan down with him as he hit the ground, covered from gunfire by the large table.

More shots rang out as Denzel started shooting at the guard, and the two of them exchanged volleys while taking cover in doorways and behind thick scraps of rotted wood shelving.

Kotler had a firm grip around Aslan's neck, and used his left hand to pat the man down, removing a small 9mm from a belt holster at the base of Aslan's back. He also found, of all things, Aslan's wallet.

He tucked that into his own pocket for now, and then used the gun to keep Aslan at bay while he backed away, flipped the large table for cover, and then peeked over to see what was happening.

"Kill them both!" Aslan shouted.

Kotler shook his head, disgusted. "Shut up, Aslan, you've already lost this fight."

"You think?" Aslan grinned. "I still control the only way off of this island."

"For now," Kotler said, then peeked back over the table's edge.

The mercenary had a pretty defensible position, in facing down Denzel. But Kotler might actually be able to clip him from his vantage point. He took aim and fired two rounds.

The first ricocheted from the stone wall behind the mercenary. The second buried itself in the rotting wood of the shelving the man used for cover.

The guard turned his attention to Kotler then, and laid down fire that bore into the thick wood of the table. Kotler ducked with a curse, staying low. Aslan did the same, further cementing Kotler's conclusion that Aslan wasn't actually in charge after all.

Denzel used the break to make an advance into the room, rushing the mercenary while firing to provide his own cover.

The guard was highly trained, however. He was able to return fire, even with Denzel's barrage buzzing all around him. He ducked low, took aim, and was peppering the walls and shelves with rounds. Denzel had to halt his approach and roll for cover just as a swarm of bullets dissolved a nearby wooden case into splinters.

When the mercenary dropped low, it gave Kotler a better shot. And he took it.

He fired three rounds, each this time hitting their target. The guard must have been wearing kevlar under his clothing, because the hits drove him back but didn't seem to stop him. He roared in fury, however, and brought his weapon to bear on Kotler, driving round after round into the table until they started to penetrate. Kotler went flat, covering his head, but knew that any second he would be torn to shreds as well.

And then, suddenly, the thunderstorm of weapons fire stopped.

After a brief lull, Kotler cautiously peeked around the

edge of the table, and saw Denzel standing, huffing, with his rifle held at ease. The guard lay slumped against the wall, blood oozing from unseen wounds. His eyes were open, and his stare led to a blank portion of the floor, as if he were studying it while in a daze.

He was dead, and Denzel had won the day.

Kotler looked then to see that some time during the fire-fight, Aslan had ducked away.

"Aslan's gone," Kotler said.

"He ran for the door," Denzel said. "I couldn't stop him at the time."

"We have to get back to that basecamp before *he* does," Kotler said. "Or we're going to live in Atlantis from now on."

CHAPTER 19

ATLANTIS ISLAND

TREKKING IN TO THE CITY HAD BEEN ARDUOUS AND difficult, but rushing through the jungle forest at top speed was worse by far. Kotler and Denzel ducked branches and vines, and occasionally had to stop and find the path again. The humidity had them both drenched, and progress seemed frustratingly slow.

There was no way to know how far ahead Aslan might be. If he reached the base camp with enough of a lead, he could have the rest of his men on top of them in no time. There were still three armed and well-trained mercenaries back at that camp, and they were fresh for the fight.

They came to yet another obstacle—a tree blocking the path, along with a thick and impenetrable tangle of vines. They would have to navigate around it to continue.

Kotler huffed and said, "This isn't going to work. Aslan has too much of a lead—we don't even know for sure which direction he went."

"You have another idea?" Roland asked, panting.

Kotler thought for a moment, letting his mind wander and putting things together in such a way that he might actually figure something out. There *had* to be a way out of this, even if they couldn't catch Aslan before he boarded the plane and left.

What had Kotler seen? What was tickling part of his brain, refusing to go away?

The mercenaries.

Aslan had been Kotler's captive, but the mercenary guarding them hadn't cared. He fired anyway, nearly killing Kotler *and* Aslan.

It wasn't the first hint that Aslan actually wasn't *in charge* of all of this. But it did cement the fact.

Which meant that Aslan was on a mission for someone else, and had *failed*. He hadn't retrieved the Atlantis treasure at all. And the first act of one of the mercenaries was to try to *eliminate* him.

Aslan was a pawn.

"I've been an idiot," Kotler said sourly.

For once, Denzel didn't leap to agreement, which was an indication of how much trouble he assumed they were in. "What've you got?"

"Aslan," Kotler said. "He isn't going back to the base camp."

"What? How do you know?"

"Because if he goes there, he's a dead man. He's a dead man either way, I think, but I'm sure he's going to avoid it as long as possible. He's not going back to camp, because if he turns up empty handed those mercenaries are going to kill him."

"Don't they work for him?" Denzel asked.

Kotler shook his head, and lifted his shirt tail to wipe his brow and clear sweat and grime from his vision. "He's a pawn. There's someone else pulling the strings."

Denzel looked off in the direction they had been moving,

moments earlier. He shook his head and snorted derisively. "It's her, isn't it."

Kotler inhaled sharply and let it out in a quick huff. "Yeah. I think so. I'm about 99% sure that Gail McCarthy is behind all of this."

"How long have you known?" Denzel asked as they continued to push through the brush, though this time at a far more cautious pace. They were in no hurry now. Removing Aslan as a threat changed the game. Wherever he might have run to, he was hiding, not trying to find his way back.

"Probably as long as you have," Kotler said.

Denzel nodded. "I started putting the pieces together when they separated us. Gail … she was constantly under some kind of duress, but always out of sight. And I started thinking, who benefits the most from finding this treasure? Van Burren is dead, which eliminates him as both a suspect and as a player in this. Aslan—whatever his real name is—clearly has no real authority, I could see that. No one else even knows about all of this. Gail, though … she had so much information. She was so *certain*."

Kotler felt a great sense of shame. He had been completely taken in by Gail, falling for everything she'd done, following everywhere she'd pointed. "She showed up in the parking garage of my apartment building," Kotler said. "She has an apartment there, so it never occurred to me that it might have been a setup. Now I wonder how long she's lived there—I've never seen her in the building."

"So Gail comes to you to, what, use you to solve all of this?"

"She's been following everything that happened in Pueblo, with the Coelho Medallion," Kotler said. "It must have triggered a plan."

"So her grandfather reveals the whole story about finding

the map and the stone, and when he dies everything comes to her. She manipulates everyone into bringing her right to the treasure."

"Only there is no treasure," Kotler said "Not here."

"And where is it, then? We know that Van Burren has been looting this island for decades. The coffers were getting light, though. He needed a bigger score, and getting to it meant solving this riddle. But there isn't anything here. So where is it?"

"Edison," Kotler said.

"What? He's been dead since the thirties."

"Exactly," Kotler said. "But we know that he had a dark estate. That's how the second stone, the journal page, *all of it* came to light."

Denzel nodded. "If we can somehow make it back to civilization, I'll start digging to find the rest of that estate. But for now, we need a plan for when we get back to that base camp. It's three armed mercenaries and your psycho girlfriend against the two of us, and we're in no shape for a firefight."

"Ok, *so* not my girlfriend," Kotler said. "And we may not have to worry about it. I'm guessing that Aslan had a check-in time, and he's missed it."

"How would you know that?" Denzel asked.

Kotler reached into his pocket, and took out Aslan's phone. He had forgotten it was there, and was only reminded about it a few seconds ago. "It started vibrating," Kotler said. He checked the display, and there was a missed call from a blocked number. He showed it to Denzel.

"Gail? Calling to get an update?"

"Most likely," Kotler said. "Which means she and the rest of the mercenaries may be on their way to the Omega site now. Or they may have cut and run."

"Fifty-fifty," Denzel said. "And either way, not good odds for us."

"Except we have a satellite phone," Kotler said, smiling. "We can call for help, at least. If we can avoid being shot by Gail's men, we stand a chance of getting off of this island."

Denzel nodded and held out a hand. Kotler handed him the phone, and the two of them found an open spot where Denzel made the call. He arranged for a rescue, along with several well-armed men of his own. It would take a few hours, but there were US troops in the general region.

"All we have to do now is stay alive," Denzel said.

"We should move off of the path," Kotler said. "Get deeper into the jungle. If Gail's men are coming this way, we can hide from them as they pass. Wait them out."

Denzel looked around them, inspecting their options. "I think we're not far from the Alpha site," he said.

Kotler thought about this. Denzel had returned the phone to him, and now Kotler used it to pull up the photo of the satellite image. He studied it for a moment "It's hard to say. We were moving in that general direction, but I can't readily identify where we are now."

"We should keep moving then," Denzel said. "We need to find at least *one* landmark, so we can tell our guys where to find us."

Kotler nodded, tucked the phone away, and the two of them started their trudge forward once again.

Nearly two hours passed before the path opened slightly and they saw the Alpha site. It was a small set of stone structures, nearly overrun by the jungle. The buildings here were more or less intact, but nowhere near the condition of the larger Omega site. They could shelter here, however. It would make a good place to hide out until their rescue arrived.

They made their way to a structure that was more or less

stable, with walls and an arching doorway. The roof had long ago collapsed into large chunks of rubble on the floor, and Denzel and Kotler rested on part of this debris, catching their breath.

"This is why I got out of the military," Denzel said, huffing.

Kotler laughed and smiled. "This? I've been in denser jungle than this."

"Voluntarily," Denzel said, shaking his head. "I'll never understand archaeologists." He thought for a moment, then asked, "Why archeology, by the way? You have a background in physics. Why not that?"

Kotler thought about it for a moment. "I pursued that, for awhile. That was one of my first passions. I wanted to know how the universe worked, from the pixels up. But the deeper I dug, the less satisfied I was. I was seeing the *mechanics* of the universe, but I wasn't really finding the *meaning*. For that, I needed to look at history. But I became bored with dates and grocery lists of fallen empires. I started looking closer at the odd bits and pieces out there. The cultures that have disappeared, and the lost arts and sciences they took with them. I started looking at the out-of-place history that was out there confusing everyone. That became my greatest interest, I guess. I decided I wanted to understand humanity, and the best way to do that was to look at the riddles we've all left sitting around."

"Like underground Viking cities in Colorado," Denzel said.

Kotler grinned. "Exactly like that. And, obviously, infamous lost cities that were swallowed by the sea."

Denzel shook his head. "I've looked into your past, you know. I know about your family. I know every school you attended, and every mentor you've spent time with over the years. You like to look into the weird history of humanity, but I think you're actually *part* of it."

Kotler considered this, nodding. "Probably," he said. "Like attracts like, after all."

They sat in silence for a moment, resting, but became alert when they heard sound from the jungle.

They exchanged glances, and then silently took up arms and found defensible positions.

Kotler had hoped they would avoid any conflict here—that perhaps they could just wait out whatever was happening on the island. If Gail and her men *were* making their way to the temple, they would bypass this site. And if they had abandoned the island altogether, Kotler and Denzel would just wait for rescue and be back in civilization in a few hours.

But it was starting to look like Gail and her men had found them after all, and they might just have to defend their position until help finally arrived.

They had their rifles trained on the tree line. From their position, they had good cover—stones four feet thick, and no way for anyone to flank them. They also had a very good view of one of the only paths into the site. They waited. Kotler squeezed the trigger to its friction point, just short of firing.

Suddenly, a man stumbled from the forest, falling face-first to the cleared ground. He scrambled back to his feet, and wiped at his face with the sleeve of his shirt.

Aslan.

Kotler felt his forearm tense. He was very tempted to squeeze the trigger past that friction point, to put a bullet into Aslan and end him as a nuisance. But he couldn't allow that. He couldn't take this man's life out of irritation alone. Aslan posed literally no threat to them, at this moment. He was, in fact, completely vulnerable.

Kotler glanced over to see Denzel, staring at him intently, waiting, as if to ask, *Will you?*

And in that look, Kotler knew that Denzel would say nothing. Kotler could pull that trigger and the only consequence would be the memory of what he had done—which was more than enough to give Kotler pause.

He eased off of the trigger, and the two of them stood and quickly made their way out into the cleared area of the site.

"Aslan," Kotler said, raising the rifle and keeping it on the man. "Do not move."

Aslan stared, his expression vacant and exhausted. He shook his head, and raised his hands, placing them on the back of his head, and then sank to his knees. "No," he said, huffing. "Moving … is the last thing … I want to do."

CHAPTER 20

ATLANTIS ALPHA SITE

THEY HAD RELAYED THE COORDINATES OF THE ISLAND
from the satellite map, but with Aslan's help they were able to
give specific directions to the Alpha site. It had taken some
time, but above them they finally heard the sound of a helicopter. It dropped to just above the tree line, and four
soldiers boiled out of it, bringing harnesses and medical
equipment with them.

Kotler and Denzel shoved Aslan ahead, his hands tied
with strips ripped from his own shirt sleeves. The soldiers
harnessed him and took him up first.

"You didn't make this easy," one of the men said to
Denzel, shouting over the sound of the rotor wash.

"We came here the hard way ourselves," Denzel shouted
back. "Did you sweep the area coming in? Any signs of an
airplane, or anyone else on this island?"

"Negative," the man said. "There's an airstrip, and we
already have one bird on the ground there. We have men
sweeping that site. We spotted the ruins you mentioned in
our flyover, but there was no one there either, and nowhere
to put down. Our people found a monitoring station in one

of the buildings near the airstrip. The men you took down were wearing body cams. The people at the base camp saw everything."

Denzel and Kotler were both being strapped in, but they exchanged looks. "That explains why we never encountered anyone," Denzel shouted.

Kotler nodded. It meant that Gail *knew*. She had watched as Kotler led them all right into that chamber. She saw instantly that there was nothing there. And she heard Kotler talk about the Edison journal—the book he'd almost forgotten, tucked into the backpack he'd lifted from one of the mercenaries.

They had worried for nothing, it seemed. But worse, Gail now knew that Edison had already retrieved the treasures from that room. And she was fully aware of the existence of his dark estate. She was ahead of them on this.

They were lifted up to the helicopter, and once inside the bird flew them back to a carrier ship off of the coast. Once there, they were given shared quarters, and a chance to shower, eat, and rest. It took half a day to get them back to the mainland, where Denzel had already arranged for transport for them and their new prisoner.

Aslan was a wreck. His demeanor—so confident and arrogant before—had devolved into something akin to a cowering puppy. He was constantly slumped, his hands always in front of him, even without the cuffs, and his eyes always downcast. Kotler recognized this as submission, and was glad to see it. Aslan might be more cooperative, if he was afraid of what was coming next.

And Kotler would need him to be cooperative, because he intended to find Gail McCarthy, and to help Agent Denzel take her and her entire operation out of play.

PART 3

CHAPTER 21

FBI OFFICES, MANHATTAN

KOTLER WAS SEATED BESIDE DENZEL AS THEY LOOKED across the table at Aslan, who was cleaned up and presentable, but dressed now in a plain jumpsuit. He'd spent the past 24 hours in a holding cell, while Kotler and Denzel were debriefed and given the opportunity to tend to their lives a bit.

Kotler hadn't wandered far from the FBI offices. He wanted his shot at interrogating Aslan, and Denzel had promised him he would have it.

Aslan was still cowering, still closed in on himself, but he'd been holding out on talking for awhile now.

Denzel had a folder with him. He tossed it on the table between them and said, "Eric Van Burren. Grandson of Robert Van Burren."

Aslan—*Eric*—said nothing, but stared at the folder.

"You orchestrated the murder of your own grandfather," Denzel said, shaking his head. "That's just cold."

"He deserved it," Eric said quietly.

Kotler watched him. At the mention of his grandfather, Eric had gotten a bit of steel in his spine. Their relationship hadn't been very loving, apparently. "He cut you out of the business," Kotler said. "Why?"

Eric looked at him, and for the first time the sadistic smile returned. "Why do you think, Dr. Kotler?"

Kotler considered this. There could be any number of reasons, but going by what Kotler had known about Van Burren, it wasn't hard to guess. "He didn't see you as worthy," Kotler said.

"He was disappointed that I never went into the military," Eric replied. "He wasn't much of a man of honor, but he did hold military service in high regard. He saw me as being in the same line as draft dodgers and washouts. But I learned the lessons of my own father, in that regard. He died in Afghanistan, trying to live up to Grandfather's standards. He would have inherited the business, and with him gone I was the natural heir. But my refusal to serve ended any chance I had." Eric made a derisive snort. "I doubt very seriously he would have let me in on the real business anyway."

"Smuggling," Denzel said. "Stealing artifacts and antiquities."

Eric laughed. "A small part of his empire, of course. There was also the gun smuggling, the drug running, the sex trade, and God knows what else."

Denzel nodded at all of this. "So you're willing to turn over his network?"

Eric smiled, "For the right deal," he said.

Kotler studied Eric for a moment. He'd known this might be the man's play, once they discovered exactly who he was. It was an attractive deal for Denzel, who had an opportunity to close a very big case that was otherwise stymied by the death of his prime suspect. Eric would have more inside information—leads that could help the FBI shut down a major smuggling operation.

But Eric Van Burren could help them with another case

as well, and that was the one Kotler was most interested in. He hated the idea of Eric somehow going free, or receiving a lighter sentence, but it would be worth it.

"What was Gail McCarthy's role in all of this?" Kotler asked.

Eric laughed. "Her *role*? She *orchestrated* it! She's been trying to get in with my grandfather for years, and damn near did. Her grandfather brought her in on all the secrets surrounding this, years ago. And since then Gail has worked to try to get into the inner circle. She wanted a cut of the business. When Edward died, she saw her opportunity."

"She kept the stone," Kotler said, "as leverage."

"That and a lot more. Don't be fooled, Dr. Kotler. Edward McCarthy may have started this as a more or less innocent and honorable man, but by the end he'd bought in on all of it. He knew about Grandfather's smuggling operation, and *facilitated* it. He still had deep contacts within the military. He was able to recruit from within Special Forces. As those guys came out of the shit storm of the Middle East, they were looking for ways to make more than minimum wage. McCarthy connected them to my grandfather, got them jobs doing all sorts of things. He supplied Grandfather with all the muscle he needed to keep up a world-spanning operation."

Kotler nodded as he heard this. It clicked. It made sense, based on what he knew.

Gail had somehow positioned herself as a lieutenant to her grandfather, and leveraged that position to build a mercenary force of her own, which she used to orchestrate all of this.

"And what did Gail have over you?" Denzel asked.

Eric laughed again. "My life, Agent Denzel. She *owned* me. She could have had me killed at any moment, but she needed me as a pawn. A front man. I went along at first because it seemed like the best way to take a little revenge on my grandfather, but by the end I was just trying to survive."

Denzel was jotting down all of this in his notebook, along with everything else. Over the next two hours they grilled Eric Van Burren for everything he knew. A deal was made, of course, and after that Eric was far more cooperative. He told them everything, and held nothing back.

Kotler and Denzel left him to the guards, who took him back to his cell while they regrouped in Denzel's office.

The blinds were closed.

"Do we trust him?" Kotler asked.

Denzel shook his head. "I don't think he has any reason to lie, at this point. I have plenty of leads to chase down regarding Van Burren's smuggling operation, but there's a problem."

"You don't have anything on Gail McCarthy."

"Not much, at any rate. Nothing that would put her away for long. At this point it's her word against Eric Van Burren's. She has no blood on her hands, that we can prove. And technically she hasn't stolen anything, since she left the island without any treasure."

Kotler shook his head. "I just can't believe it. She completely took me in. I ..." he sighed and rubbed his eyes with his right hand.

"She fooled me too, Dan," Denzel said. "But we can't let that get to us. We have to figure out her next move, and we have to figure out what to do about her. I can't arrest her. I have nothing on her."

Kotler nodded. "Right. I know. You're right." He thought for a long moment, with Denzel leaning back and staring at the door of the office. After a few minutes, Kotler sat up a little straighter and said, "We know what she's after."

Denzel nodded. "Right. But we don't know where it is, and neither does she."

"But I think she does," Kotler said.

Denzel gave him a quizzical look.

"She had a photo of the Edison stone. Dr. Rodham's stone. It was the only photographic evidence of it, and she had it."

"And Rodham got it from the dark estate," Denzel said.

"I think he got to it before she had a chance to," Kotler said. "I think she got her hands on that photo as part of some sort of inventory. She claimed she had a private investigator, which may have been true. But she couldn't have that photo in her possession unless she knew where the dark estate might be located."

Denzel leaned forward and tapped on his computer's keyboard. "Dr. Rodham is still under watch by agents outside of his home."

"He did manage to buy at least one item from Edison's dark estate," Kotler said.

"Looks like we should ask the good doctor to make a house call," Denzel replied.

CHAPTER 22

BALTON RESTAURANT, MANHATTAN

THINGS HAD CHANGED FOR DR. RODHAM SINCE KOTLER and Denzel had last encountered him. For starters, he now had two armed security personnel with him at all times. They flanked him even now, as Rodham sat on the far side of the restaurant table.

Balton had recently become one of the hottest restaurants in the city, and it was nearly filled to capacity. The crowds made it a perfect place to meet if you were uncertain of the intentions of the other party—or if you were afraid that there might be dangers unaccounted for, as had happened at Van Burren's estate.

This marked another change in Rodham's behavior, Kotler noted. Previously Rodham had used Habbersham Abbey as an intimidation tool, arranging meetings there so that he could remain in control of every nuance of the conversation. Now he was changing venues, flying into Manhattan, making the meetings as public as possible.

Rodham had been severely shaken by the experience at Van Burren's estate, and he was taking no chances from here out.

"Have you brought me here so you could return my property?" Rodham asked.

"I'm afraid that's still evidence in our investigation," Denzel replied.

"Of course it is," Rodham said. "You took it under false pretenses and threatened me if I didn't cooperate, so I'm certain it's still *vital* to your *investigation*."

"We put it to good use at least," Kotler said, smiling. Rodham gave him a look that Kotler was certain the man meant to be absolutely *withering*. He was in no way pleased with how things had turned out, obviously. And though Kotler wasn't particularly worried, he knew that Rodham was far from toothless. The man held fairly significant political sway, and should he choose, he could make life hell for Denzel, at the very least.

But Kotler was far from immune, himself. He might see some difficulties arise in dealing with museums and universities. Or he could find himself suddenly on a no-fly list, or any number of other acts of vengeance from a politically connected man.

It was best to treat Rodham with respect.

"Dr. Rodham," Denzel said, "as you know, this investigation is ongoing, and involves an item you purchased by auction from Thomas Edison's so called 'dark estate.' We would like your help in tracking down the person or persons managing that estate."

Rodham let out a bark of laughter. "You can't seriously believe I would have that information," he said. "I make my acquisitions through a third-party service. You're welcome to contact *them*."

Denzel nodded and took out his notepad. "And who are they?"

"Baker-Tait. They're the auction broker I use for all of my acquisitions. They approached me with photos and information about the Edison stone, and I authorized its purchase."

Denzel noted all of this. "I'll touch base with them then," he said.

The conversation from that point centered mostly around Denzel digging for more information about Rodham's acquisitions, whether he'd picked up anything else from the Edison estate, and whether he knew of any other buyers. Rodham cooperated, though his attitude was belligerent. He was trying to get this over with as quickly as possible so that he could retreat back to the safety of the Abbey. But ultimately he knew very little.

It became clear that Rodham was not going to be of any real help, and so Denzel told him he was free to leave. Rodham rose quickly from his chair, assisted by one of his guards, and the two burly, armed men flanked him on his way out of the restaurant.

Kotler watched them go, and shook his head. "We could have gotten that information with a phone call," he said.

"I was hoping maybe you would pick up on something Rodham might be hiding, if we met here in person," Denzel said.

Kotler shook his head. "No. He was agitated and afraid, and angry of course. But he wasn't hiding anything that I could determine."

Denzel nodded, closed his notebook, and slid it back into the pocket of his coat. "So far I hate this case," he said.

Kotler chuckled. "Oh come on, Roland. You love this, admit it. We're on a high adventure!"

"We're mired in red tape and firewalls," Denzel replied. "I've had requests in for days, asking for anything I can get on Edison's estates. It's pretty clear someone in the Bureau knows about the 'dark estate,' but there's not much information beyond that."

"So now we contact Baker-Tait," Kotler said, nodding. "This could take awhile."

Denzel was about to respond to that when Kotler's phone rang. He looked at the number and recognized it—one of Eloi Coelho's people. Kotler looked at Denzel, holding up the phone, and Denzel nodded.

"Dan Kotler," Kotler answered.

"Dr. Kotler, this is Antonia Veranza. I was one of Dr. Coelho's aides. We met once at his home."

"Antonia, yes I remember you! Is everything alright? How is Dr. Coelho?"

There was a brief silence from the other end of the phone, and Antonia said in a slightly quavering voice, "I'm calling to tell you that Dr. Coelho passed earlier this morning."

Kotler sat, silent, gripping the phone. The news must have registered on his face, because Denzel leaned forward slightly, concerned. "What's happened?" he asked in a whisper.

Kotler slowly held up a hand, asking Denzel to wait just a moment. "I'm so sorry to hear that, Antonia," he said, a bit shaken. "I appreciate you calling to let me know. Have arrangements already been made?"

"His funeral is in six days," Antonia said. "He has family in Portugal, and they are flying in. I … I've been handling the arrangements."

Kotler could hear the strain and stress in her voice, and his heart broke even further. "Antonia, I'm going to have someone contact you in the next half hour. She's a friend of mine who is wonderful at organizing things like this. I will cover all of her fees and expenses, but I want you to allow her to help you."

There was a sniffle from the other end of the phone, "I appreciate that, Dr. Kotler. Thank you."

"And I will be at Dr. Coelho's service," Kotler said. "If there's anything else I can do in the meantime, please call me."

She thanked him again, and the two hung up.

Kotler sat and stared at the phone in his hand for a moment, silent.

Denzel raised a hand, waiving, and a waiter eventually approached them. "Two scotches," he said. "Top shelf."

The waiter nodded and left.

"Drinking on duty?" Kotler asked, forcing a smile.

"I went off duty the second you got that phone call," Denzel said.

CHAPTER 23

BAKER-TAIT AUCTION HOUSE, MANHATTAN

THE FACILITY WHERE BAKER-TAIT OPERATED ITS DAY-TO-day business was not nearly as grand as some of the auction houses Kotler had visited in the past. And yet, somehow, it seemed far more upscale than any of the others. There were touches of art everywhere, which helped. But there was also a subtle sophistication to the design and flow of the building that made quite an impression.

"We operate with a very small footprint," said Bianca Miles, the General Manager. "A large portion of our work is done online, with representatives traveling all over the world. So we have very little need for a large facility."

"So much for Edison's dark estate being housed here," Denzel whispered.

Kotler understood his disappointment, but he hadn't expected this to be the end of the road. He wasn't certain what Edison's dark estate would contain, but he was certain it would be too grand to be housed in a place like this.

They were led through the facility on a sort of impromptu tour, with Bianca answering any questions that either of them had. Several minutes later, with the tour complete, they came to an office. "Morgan Keller is our head of acquisitions. She would be the most likely person to answer your questions."

"We appreciate your cooperation in this," Denzel said, smiling.

Bianca returned the smile with a coy expression of her own.

Kotler raised his eyebrows, grinning slightly at Denzel as Bianca turned to knock on the door. Denzel shot him a dirty look, and Kotler smirked.

Bianca waited a moment, then knocked again. No answer.

"Morgan?" she called, leaning toward the door, listening.

She tried the handle, and the door opened smoothly until bumping something on the other side.

Denzel gently moved Bianca back, and drew his weapon. He nudged the door with the toe of his shoe, and peeked cautiously inside. He swore, holstered his weapon, and then pushed the door wide enough to allow entry.

Kotler followed close behind, and saw immediately that they were not the first to have tracked down Morgan Keller.

"Oh my God," Bianca whispered, putting a hand to her mouth. "Morgan."

The woman lay sprawled on the floor, just inside the office door, with her head at an odd angle. Her eyes were open, and her expression was one of fear.

Kotler stooped to examine her closer. "She was strangled," he said. "Judging by the ligature marks on her neck, I'd say they used some sort of cord." He looked up and pointed, "The power cord from that lamp," he said, pointing at a lamp that lay smashed on the floor. "The bruising looks to be a few hours old."

"You're a forensics expert now?" Denzel asked.

"It's a helpful skill for my work," Kotler said.

Denzel shook his head and looked around the office as Kotler got to his feet. Everything was disheveled. "Place has been searched," Denzel said.

"I should call the police," Bianca said from the door. Kotler looked to see that she was pale and shaken.

"Do that," Denzel told her. "Tell them the FBI is on scene."

Bianca left to make the call, and Kotler and Denzel continued to look around the crime scene.

"Don't touch anything," Denzel said.

"Wouldn't dream of it," Kotler replied.

Using his pen, Denzel prodded papers and objects that were scattered on Morgan's desk, on the shelves lining one wall, even on the floor. "Whatever Morgan may have had, it's gone now," Denzel said, sighing.

Kotler was examining the edges of the desk, and took note of something. "Here," he said, pointing. "A power cable for a laptop."

Denzel nodded. "Makes sense they would take her computer."

"Places like this have very high security," Kotler said. "You should ask your girlfriend if they have a way to track the laptop, and to look at the last access it had."

"Don't even start with the girlfriend thing," Denzel grumbled. He took his phone out of his coat pocket and called the front desk, asking to be patched through to Bianca's office. He chatted with her for a moment, calming her first, and then asking her to have Baker-Tait's IT department do some digging and report the results to him.

After hanging up, he and Kotler took one more sweep of the office, then closed the door behind them as they exited, waiting in the hall until a few blue uniforms arrived, followed soon after by a detective, who was already on guard over the FBI being present.

"Detective Peter Holden," the man said, showing his badge. "You're the ones corrupting my crime scene?"

"We're the ones allowing you on *our* crime scene," Denzel said. "But let's hold off on jurisdiction bickering for a second. I'm going to bow out of this and let you take on the investigation …"

"How generous of you," Holden said.

"… but I have a related investigation that's ongoing. The IT department here is tracing something for me, and I need to dig into them before you do."

"If it's pertinent to this case …" Holden started.

"It is," Denzel interrupted. "And it's yours. But your murderer is tied to multiple homicides and a major smuggling operation. I can't risk losing any advantages."

Holden studied Denzel for a moment, as Kotler watched in fascination. He'd been a part of numerous criminal investigations in his life—on all sides, if he was being honest. But he'd never been present during a face-off between the FBI and a NYPD Detective before. It was fascinating.

"Could you use 24 hours?" Holden asked.

"Forty-eight would be better," Denzel replied. "And in return, I'll pass anything and everything I uncover on to you, as long as it doesn't jeopardize my investigation, or national security."

Holden scoffed. "That's a broad blanket," he said.

"The broadest," Denzel agreed. "But you have my word, Detective, I want this murder solved as much as you do."

He shared everything that he and Kotler had uncovered then, which admittedly wasn't much. "And I have a suspect for you to investigate," Denzel said. "Though I'm pursuing her directly myself."

"So hold off on approaching her," Holden nodded.

"Gail McCarthy," Denzel said. "You can dig into her past

all you like, but I can save you the trouble. She's the grand-daughter of Edward McCarthy, the real estate mogul."

"He died recently," Holden said. "And his partner was murdered. This have anything to do with that?"

"Everything," Denzel said. "We believe Gail McCarthy is behind all of it, but we don't have much evidence at the moment."

"Which is why you need me to play this close to my vest," Holden said.

Denzel nodded.

"Ok, Agent Denzel. You have the full cooperation of the NYPD, I personally guarantee it."

"And the FBI is at your service," Denzel said.

"And who's this guy?" Holden nodded toward Kotler.

Kotler was about to introduce himself, but Denzel interrupted, saying, "He's a consultant. He's helping me in the investigation."

Kotler put his hands in his pockets and kept his lips pressed. If Denzel didn't want his name in the mix, Kotler was more than willing to trust the play.

They chatted for a few minutes more, exchanged business cards, and then went their separate ways. Denzel was checking email on his phone as they left the Baker-Tait offices. "I have the information from IT," he said.

"Does it help?" Kotler asked.

Denzel nodded. "We have the last search from Morgan Keller's laptop, and they're pinging it continuously to see if it pops online at some point."

"What was Morgan searching for?" Kotler asked.

"Exactly what we'd hoped," Denzel smiled, turning the phone so Kotler could see. "Anything on this list set off any bells for you?"

The search results included several warehouses in the

region, from New York, New Jersey, and Connecticut, but one in particular caught Kotler's eye.

"Glenmont," he said.

"Glenmont? Where is that?"

"It's the name of Edison's estate. His *actual* estate, in West Orange."

"New Jersey? Isn't that where Edison's home and labs were?" Denzel asked.

"I'd call that a lead," Kotler said, smiling.

Denzel nodded, and the two of them walked to where Denzel's car was parked.

"I just have one question," Kotler said. "Why didn't you want Detective Holden to know my name?"

Denzel shrugged. "It's always good to keep some information close to your chest," he said. "I didn't want him spending any time looking into you, finding out what your role was in all of this. But honestly, I always try to know a little more than the police. Call it a hold card."

Kotler considered this. "So it's petty."

"Well that's rude," Denzel said. "But yes."

They drove away as Kotler grinned.

CHAPTER 24

THOMAS EDISON NATIONAL HISTORICAL PARK, NEW JERSEY

THEY DROVE FROM MANHATTAN TO ESSEX COUNTY, which gave Kotler plenty of time to relax a bit, and let everything he'd experienced over the past few months drift into the background as he stared at the shifting scenery.

He needed the mental break, actually. The news of Dr. Coelho's death still lingered with him, reminding him of mortality, and of the fleeting time every human has with friends and family.

Kotler's specialty was history—of late, the sort of out-of-place history that creates intriguing mysteries to be solved. It was work he loved, though it did give him a unique perspective on life and death. There was a sort of *distance* to it.

He was used to the idea of death and mortality, as a concept. But studying the remains of people and cultures that had been dead for thousands of years was little preparation for the loss of someone you *knew*. It made Kotler pause to evaluate his life, and to wonder if in his quest to understand the world and the universe, maybe he was looking past too many details. Maybe he needed to spend a little more time considering the *living*.

His thoughts drifted to Evelyn Horelica.

He hadn't spoken to her in some time now. In fact, their last communication had been by email, months ago, as this entire Atlantis affair had begun. Kotler realized with a start that he had stopped reaching out to Evelyn around the same time that he'd met Gail McCarthy.

Was he really that fickle? That easily distracted?

He and Evelyn had been lovers for a time, but things had cooled somewhat just before she took a position in Houston. The move had separated them physically, but for awhile there it seemed to give them a boost emotionally. Distance had made the heart grow fonder, it seemed to Kotler. They had teased each other, flirted with each other, and continued to bond with each other over emails and text messages and Skype calls. When they saw each other in person, the old flames ignited, and things were good again. And then Evelyn returned to Houston and Kotler returned to Manhattan—or Borneo, or Egypt, or Moscow or any number of other places where his work was in progress. This sort of checking-in seemed to work for them as a couple.

And then Evelyn had been kidnapped and held hostage, in connection with the theft of the Coelho Medallion and everything that Mark Cantor and Anwar Adham had orchestrated. After that, the connection between Kotler and Evelyn had become too strained. Their relationship became a series of emails, and those were guarded, unemotional.

Kotler mourned for the loss of connection with Evelyn. He missed her. He missed their in-jokes and their barely masked attraction.

Maybe that's why I was so easy to fool, Kotler thought. Gail McCarthy was an attractive and winsome woman, with a sharp intelligence and a taste for adventure. Perhaps in her Kotler had seen some of Evelyn, but with the added bonus of having a companion who was not afraid to pursue the mysteries of the world, right alongside him. Maybe Gail McCarthy had represented someone who could fill in the gaps of Kotler's life, and that's why he'd been so blind to her.

Maybe that's why he'd been such a fool.

It was a few hours after leaving the FBI's Manhattan offices that Kotler and Denzel arrived at Glenmont—Edison's remaining estate, now preserved as a national park site.

Glenmont itself was a large, red-bricked home that embodied the very industrial nature one would expect from Thomas Edison. From the drive leading to the house, Kotler could see dozens of windows, multiple chimneys, even a covered area where Edison and guests would be able to exit one of Ford's miraculous motorized coaches, safe from rain or other nasty weather. Kotler could envision all of it in his mind, and experienced a sense of longing for it. He'd pay real money to be able to look back into the past with clarity, rather than through the hazy lens of archeological discovery all the time.

It was a rare treat, however, to be able to see some history intact and preserved.

Glenmont was now part of the Thomas Edison National Historical Park—a preservation of Edison's home and laboratory in Llewellyn Park, West Orange. As a National park, it had been remarkably well preserved, with the sprawling grounds still playing home to Edison's multiple laboratory buildings. It was a large complex of hiding places, from Kotler's perspective. Edison's dark estate could be hidden in any of them. But at least they had something of a lead.

As they arrived and entered the main building, they met with Evan Scott, the Managing Curator for the park. Denzel had called ahead to arrange the meeting, and Evan was more than happy to chat with them. He was younger than Kotler would have expected, considering his position as curator. He had the air of someone who was doing a job he mostly loved, but who had clearly wanted something just a bit different from his career. Despite this, however, Evan's attitude and demeanor was very positive and affirming, and Kotler found he liked the man.

"We need access to the warehouse mentioned in this document," Denzel said, handing Evan a printout of the information provided by Baker-Tait.

Evan peered at the document, squinting a bit. "I forgot my glasses," he said, smiling up at them before pulling the sheet closer. He was a young, fit-looking man—with the bearing of someone who enjoyed the outdoors. Kotler figured he must have joined the National Park Service hoping to spend time in forests and among nature, but had somehow managed to land a role preserving an iconic part of national history instead. He didn't seem to mind, from Kotler's observation. He was a personable and happy guy who likely went kayaking on the weekends.

"This is the garage," he said finally. "It was converted into climate controlled storage several years ago. We store Edison artifacts there that we occasionally rotate out for display."

Denzel took out his phone and brought up images of the Atlantis stones. "Have you ever seen anything like this among the items in storage?" he asked.

Evan looked at the phone, zooming in with a pinch to examine things closer. "There was a stone like this in the basement," he said.

Denzel nodded. "We're going to need access to that basement," he said.

Evan showed them the way to the garage, which stood near the main house but was its own separate structure.

It looked less like a garage, and more like a firehouse, in Kotler's estimate. It was a two-story structure with numerous windows, and a large, arching doorway. The drive wound directly to this, and they followed the path until they came to the enormous doors. "The real garage door was damaged beyond repair," Evan said. "So during the restoration, this new door was added." He lifted the cover of a small panel to the right of the door and entered a code. Immediately the large door rolled up and out of the way, revealing that it was actually a series of cleverly disguised panels.

They entered the space, and Kotler was immediately struck by the presence of so much history.

Everywhere he looked there were hundreds of objects and artifacts, all perfectly preserved. Many items were covered, to prevent dust and light from damaging them. But a great many more stood freely in the open, where they could be observed and admired by anyone coming through. They were clearly cared for—all of the brass and wood and leather was polished and immaculate. Kotler smiled as they walked past inventions and laboratory equipment that defied description.

"You have that 'kid in a candy store' look," Denzel said.

"I'm just impressed by the industriousness and ingenuity of the place," Kotler replied, his features lit with the joy of experience.

"This way to the basement," Evan said, also smiling.

"You have an amazing collection here," Kotler said.

"You'll have to come back and take the full tour some time," Evan nodded. "There are some amazing exhibits here. And look me up, I'd be happy to give you a personal tour."

Kotler also nodded, aware suddenly that Evan was hitting on him. And though Kotler was not inclined toward the type of relationship Evan might have wanted, he didn't have the heart to shoot down any hopes at the moment. He looked up and caught a quick smirk from Denzel. He'd take flack later, he knew.

They were led through a short and narrow corridor that brought them to an iron staircase, which spiraled up into the ceiling and down into the floor. "This is one of two entrances. There's a freight elevator on the far end of the garage, but this is closer. And I kind of like it, actually."

They took the stairs, single file, and descended into the basement. Lights clicked on as they entered, triggered by motion sensors. When they got to the floor, they stood and looked at shelf upon shelf of cataloged and organized bins, trays, and unidentified objects.

"Welcome to the basement," Evan said, making a grand, sweeping gesture with his hands. "I know, a bit dramatic. But I never get to show anyone this place."

"Could you show us where the stone would have been stored?" Denzel asked.

"Right this way," Evan said.

He led them through row after row of shelving, until they came to the very back of the space, where a large, meshed cabinet stood. There was a padlock in place, to keep anyone from casually opening the door. Peeking in through the metal grating, Kotler could see a few odds and ends.

"These are some items Edison and his people brought back from expeditions. Some of these haven't been identified yet. We keep all of it under lock and key because we had some thefts a few years ago."

"Was the stone stolen during that time?" Denzel asked.

Evan nodded. "Along with a few other odds and ends. The inventory of this cabinet was stolen as well. Which makes things difficult."

"You couldn't report something stolen if you didn't know it existed," Denzel said.

"Exactly. It was a bit before my time, but I got to hear the whole story from the previous curator."

"Can we take a look at what's inside the cabinet?" Denzel asked.

Evan nodded, took a set of keys form his pocket, and opened the padlock.

Inside, Kotler saw numerous cultural artifacts. There were samples of materials as well—something Edison was famous for. He was on a continuous quest to find the perfect materials to suit the inventions coming out of his labs.

In his quest to invent the light bulb, for example, he had scoured the earth looking for various materials that might do the trick for a filament. He ultimately settled on a carbon-enriched bamboo fiber, but only after experimenting with *thousands* of other possibilities.

He was known for using that same practice with the rest of his work, meticulously recording his findings in notebooks.

There were many interesting items in the cabinet, but nothing that really set off any bells for Kotler.

Denzel looked at him, quizzically.

"Sorry," Kotler shrugged. "I'm not seeing anything that really ties in."

"So are we sure this is the place, then?" Denzel asked. "Would Edison's dark estate be here?"

Kotler shook his head. "I don't think it would be this obvious," he said. "The fact that the stone was out in the open seems like an anomaly. If Edison really did clean out that temple, he wouldn't have kept it out in the open for just anyone to see. He would have stored it away in secret."

"I'm sorry," Evan Scott said. "Did you say 'dark estate?'"

They turned to him.

"It's just … rumors of that have been going around for years," he said. "Most of them are pretty out there. But …"

"What is it?" Denzel asked.

"When I took over, the previous curator told me that there was more to the garage than anyone knew. He said there was a chamber somewhere in here, hidden. A vault, actually."

"Did he say where?" Denzel asked.

Evan shook his head. "No. Which is why I figured he was just messing with me."

"Who else knows about it?" Kotler asked.

"I can't say for sure. It's been a rumor around here since well before I started. We had a groundskeeper who suddenly came into a lot of money and retired, several years ago, and the rumor was that he'd found the vault, but couldn't really get into it. He'd only been able to sneak a few things out, they say, but had to leave the rest. He was a suspect in the theft of the stone, though."

Kotler and Denzel exchanged looks, then Denzel asked, "Where can we find the groundskeeper?"

"He died a couple of years ago," Evan said. "I'm sorry."

"It's fine," Kotler said, looking around at the basement. "I have an idea."

"Something I'll regret, no doubt," Denzel said.

Kotler smiled, but denied nothing.

Kotler stood as close to the center of the basement as he could. He peered up at the high ceilings and hoped there was enough headroom for what he was about to do.

The equipment had arrived within two hours of his call, and he had spent half an hour setting up. Denzel had not been patient during all of this.

"Is there any chance we'll actually get this done before we become one of the exhibits in this place?"

Kotler smiled, and lifted the controls—a smart tablet mounted to a box with two control sticks. The grips were shaped for his palms, and the two control sticks would control altitude and attitude. The controls worked the mini-drone, which in turn acted as a platform for the Lidar array.

"We're set," Kotler said.

Evan Scott stood at Denzel's side, nervously chewing his fingernails. "You're sure that you're going to be able to control it? If it damages any of these artifacts …"

"I'm sure, Evan," Kotler smiled, reassuringly. "I've done this many times before."

Evan nodded, and Kotler touched the controls on the tablet, which activated the drone's four spinning propellers.

The buzz was obnoxiously loud in the enclosed space of the basement, and Kotler wished he'd thought to use ear plugs. Denzel and Evan both had their fingers in their ears.

The drone rose from the floor of the basement, then hovered above the tops of the racks in the room. Kotler watched it, adjusting the controls until he had it hovering as close to the ceiling as he dared. He touched the controls for the Lidar array then, and watched as the display changed from a standard camera view to the neon hues of the Lidar imaging. The screen was mostly black for a moment, but within seconds a green-tinted landscape began to appear, gaining details with each sweep of the Lidar and dotted occasionally by peaks of red and valleys of blue. This was the room from above. With every pass of the lasers from the array the image became more distinct—a 3D scan of the entire room, including the three men standing within.

One of the primary advantages of this view was that it highlighted things that might go unseen by the naked eye. Kotler had used this technology to scan forests for signs of city ruins, and to scan tombs for signs of hidden passages. The latter was more appropriate in this case—and in time Kotler saw what he had hoped to find.

Near the cage, where the Edison stone had once been kept, was a pattern of stone in the floor that was clearly out of sync with the surrounding surface. Kotler saw distinct lines, well-hidden among the shelving and equipment, but accessible. There was a series of rows formed by tightly pressed bricks—like ribs of corduroy hidden in the floor.

"I think I have it!" Kotler shouted over the buzz of the drone.

Denzel and Evan looked at each other and shrugged.

Kotler grinned and shook his head, then brought the drone to a landing, letting its motors spin down. He saved the recording that had been running on the tablet, and played it back for Denzel and Evan.

"Definitely something," Denzel said. "I can't really tell what it is, though."

"I believe it's an entrance," Kotler said. "A passage to another level, below the basement."

"It's been there the whole time," Evan Scott whispered, shaking his head and then smiling. "So cool."

"We'll have to move these three racks to get to it," Kotler said, pointing. "Will that be alright?"

"It's fine," Evan said, waving. "They're on casters. We move them all the time."

Kotler nodded. "Now I just need to find the trigger, to open whatever this is."

Denzel was studying the images closely, and pointed at something on top of one of the 3D shelves. "What is that? Is that a camera?" he asked. He looked at Evan. "Do you have footage of your groundskeeper in here? Maybe we could search that to find out what he discovered."

Evan peered at the screen and shook his head, smiling. "We don't have any cameras in here. We probably should, considering, but we've never gotten around to it."

"Then what is that?" Denzel asked, leaning in close.

"That," a woman's voice said from behind them, "would belong to me."

They turned, and Kotler felt his blood go cold—though whether it was because of the four armed men aiming weapons at them, or because they were flanking Gail McCarthy, he couldn't say for sure.

CHAPTER 25

BASEMENT OF THE GLENMONT ESTATE GARAGE

"Crap," Denzel grumbled. "How many times is this lady going to get the drop on me?"

"Just this one last time, Roland," Gail smiled. "And don't feel bad about it. I've always been very patient. I waited until the right moment, that's all."

"Gail," Kotler said, his voice filled with regret. "You don't have to do this. Until this moment, there wasn't enough evidence against you. We could have worked something out."

"We never would have," Gail said, shaking her head. "Because you would always have stood between me and Atlantis."

"Looting it, yes," Kotler said. "But *discovering* it—and Edison's ties to it—couldn't that have been enough?"

She laughed. "No, sorry," she said. "The treasures of Atlantis are something I was told about my entire life, and I watched my grandfather waste every opportunity to claim it. When he died, I finally got my hands on what Richard Van Burren and I both needed."

"Van Burren?" Kotler asked. "You were working with him?"

"He may have been Eric's grandfather by blood, but he was mine by *spirit*," she smiled. "But he was also the competition."

"So you eliminated him," Kotler said, sadly.

"It was necessary," she said, shaking her head. "He spent most of his life trying to find Atlantis, and I wasn't about to pick up *that* legacy. I'm patient, but I still want to live while I'm young. Once we started uncovering Edison's dark estate and the bits of journal, all of the pieces that Edison had hidden—Van Burren didn't act. He was trying to keep his smuggling operation stable instead. As if drugs and guns and *girls* were any more valuable than the greatest treasure in *history*."

Kotler felt more than saw Denzel's weight shift. He was positioning himself just in front of Evan—a sign that he was about to act, and didn't want to risk Evan as a casualty.

The guards must have noticed too, because at once they raised and pointed their weapons at Denzel.

"Roland," Gail said, "hand over your gun, please. Slowly."

Denzel cursed under his breath and lifted his weapon with two fingers. He lowered it to the ground, and kicked it to Gail.

"Now, Dan," Gail said. "We were watching as you figured this out. And you *have* figured it out. I knew you would. I knew it from the moment I read about you and that Viking affair. It's the whole reason I bought that apartment. Let's go the rest of the way. How do we get into the vault?"

"I have no idea," Kotler said.

Gail looked at one of her mercenaries and nodded. The man stepped forward and used his weapon to nudge Denzel to the side. He then grabbed Evan, yanking the young man forward and forcing him to his knees. The mercenary placed the barrel of his weapon to Evan's head.

"Please," Evan pleaded. "Please don't!"

"Gail," Kotler said, a note of warning in his voice.

"Dan, you're the smartest man I've ever met. If anyone can figure this out, I'm confident it's you. Because you care about people. And if you don't have me in that vault within the next thirty minutes, this man is going to die right in front of you. And then we'll start the clock over with Roland."

Kotler studied her, taking in all of the body language of this woman, reading in her that she was very serious, and very determined.

How could he have missed it before? How could he have gotten her so *wrong*? He was an *expert* at body language. He could see the lies on someone's face, know when they were hiding something. But he'd been blinded by Gail—by her beauty, but also by something else. She was charming, and she was manipulative, at a level he'd never encountered before.

He turned and faced the rest of the room, examining the shelving all around them. He started moving the rolling racks of artifacts, clearing them from the space that—he hoped—was the entrance to the vault. He consulted the Lidar imaging from time to time, to assess what needed to be moved, and to find any clue as to how to open this thing.

With the racks cleared and out of the way, the ribbed pattern of the floor was a bit more visible to the naked eye. Though without knowing it was there it would be very easy to overlook.

Kotler had seen many hidden entrances in his career. There was a always a trigger nearby, usually cleverly hidden in the architecture of the room. It was typically camouflaged to look like part of a wall, or the knot in a board, or a finial of some sort. But here, in the plain and utilitarian space designed by Thomas Edison himself, there was nothing that *stood out.*

Which meant it would be something Edison alone would recognize.

One of the advantages of searching for something created by an individual of Edison's fame was that Kotler instinctively knew some of the psychology of the man. He knew that Edison was something of a showman—one of the best early marketers, really, when it came to introducing his work. He was the Steve Jobs of his day, and his 'one more thing' was always some bit of *wow* that he could use to dazzle the press and generate good buzz.

A man like that had some pride in his work. He would think of it often, as the achievement that it was.

Kotler looked around again, taking in all the details of the room.

"Evan," he said, "when this place was remodeled, was any of the original architecture left intact?"

Even was trembling. "I … I don't know," he said.

"Think, Evan!" Kotler said. "Something Edison would have built himself. Maybe the electrical system? The lights?"

"All of the lights and switches are original," Evan said. "We've replaced the bulbs, but the fixtures are the same. We had to replace the wiring, over time, to bring it up to code. But we kept the switches, out of … of nostalgia." He was cowering under the barrel of the gun as he said this, and shaking. Kotler wanted to free him, to get him out of there, but the best way to do that was to *solve this.*

He looked around and saw one of the switches mounted to a box on the walls, not far from the ribbing on the floor.

It was a round wood and brass fixture on the wall— resembling a small front desk bell from a hotel, mounted horizontally. The switch itself was a tiny little piece of brass shaped like a board game piece. On the whole it resembled a doorbell more than a modern light switch.

Kotler went to it and examined it.

If the wiring was replaced at some point, then this switch would have been removed from the wall. So the switch itself might not have anything to do with the vault. But it was the best lead Kotler had.

And besides, the groundskeeper had found his way into the vault, somehow. So whatever the key was, it had to still be present.

Kotler touched the switch, flipped it off and on a few times, which flicked the lights in this part of the warehouse. The mercenaries tensed, but Gail calmed them with a wave of her hand.

The lights had nothing to do with it, Kotler surmised. The key would have been discovered, and possibly disabled, during the rewiring. So what else could it be?

What would a groundskeeper have done that might have triggered the vault opening?

Kotler thought for a moment, then reached out and clasped the 'bell' of the switch, as if it was a doorknob. And he gave it a turn.

There was an audible series of clicks from within the wall, and then the hum of unseen electric motors from below them.

Kotler heard Gail and the others cry out, and he looked up to see them stepping back as the ribbed floor, now sinking before them, slowly transforming into a staircase that led into a darkened space below.

"Well done, Dan!" Gail said, her expression filled with genuine glee. She stared down into the expanding maw of the vault, and gave him a sly look. "Do you want to see what we've just uncovered?" She laughed, and shook her head. "Of course you do. And how could I refuse? Let's go down together, Dan. Let's go discover history."

Gail and Kotler mounted the steps together. She gave her mercenaries orders to kill Evan and Denzel, if she didn't return or if Kotler returned without her. Kotler was effectively leashed by that order, and so he went along without comment and without taking any action.

They made their way down the stairs, emerging into a cavernous room that stretched far in every direction. Kotler saw huge pistons and gears on either side of them—the machinery that opened and closed this vault. That was intriguing enough—a significant discovery tied to one of the world's most famous inventors. But it was the rest of the view that stunned Kotler the most.

Everywhere he looked, here in the vault, there were wide tables *covered* in gold and other artifacts. They formed a grid that stretched in every direction, far enough that Kotler hadn't yet seen the far end of the room. It might well go on for *miles*, judging by the darkened distance.

There were lights here—ancient looking Edison bulbs hanging from cables that dangled down from the ceiling. They had seen such infrequent use over the past hundred years that they were all still intact—pristine, functional and original creations of Edison himself. These alone were worth a fortune to the right collector.

But if they were a prize, the rest of the room was a treasure trove beyond the dreams of Avarice.

"It's ..." Gail started.

"Stunning," Kotler finished. They both stood, mouths agape, inspecting the ancient treasures closest to them. Kotler spotted several familiar symbols among the artifacts, linking them to the Atlantis find as sure as if there had been a placard in front of them.

It was clear that Edison had been studying many of the artifacts. There were journals at every table—one of Edison's charac-
teristic requirements of himself and of the men who worked for
him. He made meticulous notes about *everything*, in his effort to
learn and use that new knowledge to invent and innovate.

Which brought an intriguing possibility to the surface, as
Kotler picked up and examined the notes of one of the journals. Was Edison using the Atlantis treasure as *inspiration?*
Had Edison studied Atlantis artifacts as a *source* for some of
his inventions?

Edison was one of the most prolific patent holders on the
planet—a fact made somehow controversial by the fact that
many considered him a thief. His conflicts with Tesla, for
example, were *legendary*. But no one had ever accused him of
cribbing from ancient technology before. This was the sort of
discovery that would change history forever.

If anyone survived to talk about it.

"Gail," Kotler said, "it's not too late. You'll have to serve
some time—that's unavoidable. But I can help. Denzel and I
can try to get you a reduced sentence. We can ask for
leniency."

Gail laughed. "Dan, I appreciate that. But I won't need
it. I'm currently the wealthiest woman on the *planet*. Which
means I can be in a non-extradition country in no time,
along with my treasure. I have properties lined up in several
places around the world already. I can have a whole new
identity by this time tomorrow, if I need it. But I won't
need it."

Kotler instantly knew what that meant. "You'll have us
killed," he said.

"I don't want to," she replied, her voice softening with
real emotion. "I really didn't want it to get to this. But it did.
And ... well, it is what it is."

"There's a detective who has your name, in connection with the murder of Morgan Keller."

"That wasn't me," Gail said. "Not directly. There's nothing that will tie me to her death."

"You ordered it, Gail. That's going to come out."

She shook her head. "No," she said. "It won't."

She gestured, and then she and Kotler took to the steps again, emerging back up top, in the basement. She turned to one of the mercenaries. "Get the truck. And we'll need more. We'll do this tonight. Use the garage entrance. And if anyone asks, we have paperwork that says we're authorized to be here. It'll be signed by Evan Scott," she turned and smiled at the young man, who nodded quickly. He would have done *anything* to get out of there at that point.

The mercenary left, and the three remaining men split the duties of corralling Kotler, Denzel, and Evan into a corner of the basement, and securing the garage against any intrusion. Two of the guards left then, going to assist in arrangements to move the treasure and leaving one man behind.

Kotler sidled up to Denzel, who was staring down the armed guard. "We need a plan," Kotler whispered.

"Fresh out," Denzel said. "Other than tackling that bastard and taking his weapon."

"Dicey," Kotler said. He peered around, and let out a quick, quiet huff of laughter. "Would a distraction help?"

"Yes it would," Denzel said. "What do you have in mind?"

"Just watch for it," Kotler said.

"Quiet!" the guard shouted. "Move away from each other, now!"

Kotler held up his hands as he stepped aside, moving away from Denzel and Evan. He leaned against the caged rack of artifacts, and the guard eventually relaxed.

Kotler waited a beat before making his move, and then in one quick motion he stooped and grabbed the controls for the drone. He activated it, and the deafening buzz rose quickly as the drone lifted from the floor and into the air.

The guard turned and raised his weapon, taking aim at the drone.

Denzel rushed him, knocking him backwards onto the floor. They wrestled for a moment, and then Denzel grasped the rifle with both hands, shoving it into the mercenary's throat, hard. He pressed all of his weight there until the guard's feet kicked spasmodically. It was over quickly, and Denzel was up, with the weapon readied.

Gail had run from her place at the far end of the room at the first sounds of the drone, and Kotler assumed that at any moment the other three guards would rush in, weapons hot.

He moved the drone into position, and as soon as one of the mercenaries entered, Kotler tilted it and drove it straight into the man. Even over the raucous sound of the motors he could hear the screams as the blades torn into his neck and face.

Denzel fired then, two quick bursts that took out the injured guard and sent the second back out of the door, taking cover.

The drone's motors died down, and Kotler tossed the controls aside. He raced to Evan, who was cowering behind a rack of equipment. "Come with me!" Kotler shouted, reaching out a hand.

Evan took it, and followed Kotler back into the maze of racks and shelves. Denzel joined them, just as weapons fire started from the doorway. Bullets ricocheted from the metal shelving, whining into the far corners of the room.

They huddled for a moment, and then Denzel leapt up and returned fire.

Using the barrage as cover, Kotler dragged Evan from

their spot to another part of the room, followed quickly by Denzel.

"We won't hold them off for long," Denzel panted. "We need a way out!"

Kotler looked at Evan, "Is there an exit? Something other than the staircase?"

"The freight elevator," Evan said. "It's the only other way out!"

"They'll have that sewn up," Denzel said. "That's how they'll get that treasure out."

Kotler nodded, agreeing. But he had a thought. "Is it an open shaft? Original to the building?" he asked Evan.

"Yes," Evan said. "We had to have safety rails installed, to pass inspection, but they're easy to get past."

"Follow me!" Kotler said, and raced now toward the far side of the basement, where the elevator was likely to be.

They ducked and ran from case to case, with Denzel laying cover fire from time to time. The mercenary had taken up a position just outside of the door of the room, and he seemed prepared to wait things out if need be. Eventually, Denzel would run out of ammunition, and they'd be trapped for sure.

They got to the freight elevator, and Kotler flipped open the switch guard, hitting the up button and sending the elevator on its rising path to the next floor.

"So we're not using that to escape?" Denzel asked, concerned.

"We are, actually," Kotler said. He pointed down into the shaft, which sunk several feet below the floor line. In an instant he leapt into it, followed by Evan and Denzel.

"Now what? Wait to be crushed to death?" Denzel asked.

Kotler was feeling around the edges of the shaft, and quickly found what he was looking for. He pulled at a handle, and a panel opened up, revealing a crawl space. "Access for repair," Kotler said. "This will lead out."

"You're sure?" Evan asked, dubious. "I don't remember this."

"You likely would never have reason to know about it," Kotler said. "Trust me!"

He crawled into the space first, followed soon after by Evan and then Denzel, who closed the hatch behind them.

They were immediately cast into pitch black, and Kotler had to force himself to keep pressing forward at a quickened pace, trusting that he wouldn't smack into any obstacles or err into any sudden drops. The crawlspace rose in gradual inclines, connecting the basement to the ground floor, which made it more of a labor to move forward. It was a tense several minutes.

But it ended in an instant when he bumped into the panel on the far side of the crawlspace. He felt around, found the handle, and opened the door, swinging it outward as he and the others emerged into another space.

"This is the boiler room," Evan said, looking around in awe. "It's not used anymore. It's just storage now."

"Good," Kotler said. "We can regroup here."

They closed the hatch to the crawlspace, and barricaded it with heavy equipment from the room. Each of them was filthy at this point, covered with grime from head to toe. But they were alive.

There was a door on the far side of the room, and Kotler opened this cautiously, peering out. It led into the main space of the garage. He saw Gail waving in the fourth mercenary, who backed in a very large truck through the open garage doors.

"Well," Kotler said. "We're not quite home free."

Denzel peered through the slight crack in the door. "We can take that guard, and Gail," he said. "But the other one—

there's no way to know if he's still downstairs. We'd be risking another firefight."

"Do we have any choice?" Kotler asked.

Denzel shook his head. "We do this on three," he said. He turned to Evan, "You stay here. No matter what happens, you stay in this room. Lock and block the door behind us."

Evan nodded.

"Do you have a mobile phone?" Kotler asked.

Evan feebly pulled out his phone.

"You had that the whole time?" Denzel asked, annoyed.

"I … I forgot," Evan said. "They never searched me."

"Never mind," Kotler said. "Chalk it up to God on our side." He looked at Evan, placing a hand on his neck, calming him. "Call the police," Kotler said, then he looked up at Denzel. "On three."

"One," Denzel said, raising the rifle so that he could clear the door and take aim quickly.

"Two," he put the flat of his palm on the door.

"Three!" he shouted, and they pushed forward, racing out into the open garage with Denzel's weapon firing.

CHAPTER 26

GLENMONT ESTATE GARAGE

THEY EMERGED WITH DENZEL FIRING IN FULL AUTO AS he and Kotler ran for the opening of the garage. There were few items to provide cover, between them and the opening, and the only advantage they had for the moment was the element of surprise. That, and the fact that one of the two mercenaries was still below, cautiously prodding every hiding spot in the basement.

Kotler didn't see where Gail disappeared to, when the firefight started. He did note that the driver barely registered that he was being fired upon, and stepped up as if bullets were mere gnats for him to swat away.

This man was well trained for combat—he was brave to the point of being stupid. And he didn't shy away from the potential of being fatally hit—instead, he raised his own weapon and returned fire.

Denzel and Kotler managed to make it out of the garage as the bullets ricocheted around them, and from their new position Denzel was able to hold the man off. For now.

Despite holding a relatively protected position, they couldn't risk breaking and making a run for it, especially with the second mercenary still unaccounted for. It was better to stay in a position where they could monitor all of the exits, and keep at least one known threat pinned.

It didn't take long for the second mercenary to arrive, though, and to take up a secured position just inside the stairwell, where he couldn't quite get the firing advantage over Denzel but *could* keep things interesting.

Kotler felt useless without a weapon.

He looked around, trying to find *anything* he could use to even the odds of this fight. The police would be on their way by now, he hoped, but they might not get here in time to provide much backup. And they might not know to come armed for war.

"Can you hold them?" Kotler asked.

"You got somewhere to be?" Denzel shouted back.

"Just hold them!"

Kotler ran then, headed away from the garage and the cacophony of gunfire, ducking as bullets whizzed by his head more than once.

He had no plan. There seemed to be little he could actually do, and at any moment Denzel might be overrun by the two men he was facing. Somehow, Kotler had to even the odds.

He came to the car they'd used to drive in. This was an official car, supplied by the FBI. Denzel had locked it when they'd exited, and Kotler didn't have a key.

But he did have a paver stone.

Picking up one of the loose pavers from along the side of the drive, Kotler used it to smash through the driver-side window. He used the trunk release to pop the trunk and went to search for a tire iron or something else he might be able to use. It might not be all that effective, but it was better than facing these men completely unarmed.

He paused as he looked into the trunk.

There was a small arsenal in there, including a bullet-proof vest with the FBI insignia on it, and a riot gun, all neatly arranged for ready access.

Kotler picked up the gun and inspected it. Non-lethal rounds. It could fire either bead bags or canisters of crowd suppression gas. There were four of these canisters in a foam insert in the trunk.

Kotler grabbed the gun and canisters, loading two into the dual barrels of the gun and shoving the other two into his coat pockets. He pulled on the bullet-proof vest, cinching it up snugly to his body. It might provide just enough protection to make a difference. He hoped.

Kotler ran then for the garage, where the firefight still raged in alternating bursts.

Denzel was crouched beside the garage opening, taking quick shots at the interior, and Kotler was nearly close enough to at least lend a hand. He was about to take up position next to Denzel when he spotted movement at the far corner of the building.

Gail.

She had somehow exited the garage, and was sneaking up on Denzel, with Denzel's own handgun. Kotler took aim with the riot gun and fired one of the canisters directly into her.

She let out a scream from the impact, falling backwards and firing into the air. The tear gas enveloped her then and her scream was stifled in a fit of coughing and sputtering. Kotler saw the handgun fall to the ground as Gail stumbled and fell back, tripping over the small hedges surrounding the garage, before being enveloped in a cloud of the noxious gas.

Kotler weighed his options. He needed to get to Gail, to take her down for good, but with the gas cloud he wouldn't be able to get near her at the moment. Instead, he made the decision to end this firefight once and for all.

He plunged ahead, and before Denzel even knew he was there Kotler fired the second canister into the garage.

"Gas!" one of the men shouted, and then all Kotler heard was their sputtering and cursing. He loaded the last two canisters into the gun and fired both at different spots within, providing coverage of the entire space. He then ran and hit the controls for the door.

In seconds it was closed, and the two men were either incapacitated by the gas or otherwise out of the way.

Kotler turned to Denzel, who looked baffled.

"I broke into the toy box," Kotler said.

Denzel stared at him for a moment, and then laughed. "Just take off that vest before the police get here, ok? I'm going to take enough flak without having to cover you for impersonating the FBI."

The police arrived within fifteen minutes, and apparently Evan had managed to convey the danger of their situation. A SWAT team arrived in full combat gear, and they coordinated with Denzel before entering the garage, gas masks in place, and apprehending the two mercenaries. Both emerged with their eyes swollen shut and mucus dripping from their chins. They were treated by a medic before being hauled into the local jail, where Denzel would arrange for them to be taken into FBI custody in the morning.

Ambulances had arrived alongside police, and these took the bodies from the basement.

That left only one person unaccounted for.

"Gail must have slipped away," Kotler said, clenching his jaw and his fists. "I *had her*, Roland. I had her, and I let her get away!"

"You took out those two armed men," Denzel said. "It was a sacrifice worth making."

Kotler heard him, and understood, but wasn't entirely sure he believed it. Those were men for hire. Gail was the mastermind for all of this. With her out there, things could still get ugly.

But they would have to track her down later. For now, Kotler and Denzel were being checked over by paramedics, and were giving a debriefing to local police.

Evan was sitting on the bumper of one of the police cars, a blanket wrapped around his shoulders. The officers had questioned him, and with his statement taken he was free to go, but he had insisted on sticking around to talk to Kotler and Denzel.

"That treasure," he said. "It's … it's from *Atlantis?*"

Kotler and Denzel exchanged glances, and Denzel shrugged.

Kotler turned to Evan. "Listen … for the moment, we need to keep that quiet," he said. "We haven't confirmed anything. But … yeah."

Kotler looked at Denzel, who simply shrugged.

Evan shook his head. "Thomas Edison found Atlantis," he said quietly.

It was a statement that indicated the rethinking of certain life choices, Kotler knew. Evan Scott may have seen his assignment at the Edison estate as less than desirable before, but now he was connected to something so much bigger than he had ever imagined. Kotler could see the spark in his eyes.

"We'll need to take that into our custody of course," Denzel said. "But … the FBI would be very appreciative if you assisted us in cataloging everything that's in that vault."

"Yes!" Evan shouted, perhaps louder than he had intended. "I would be happy to do that," he said then, calmer.

Denzel smiled and nodded, and he and Kotler made their way back to Denzel's car. They stopped and looked at the smashed window, with glass all over the driver's seat. Denzel looked at Kotler, an annoyed expression on his face. "You couldn't have smashed the back window?"

"I was in a hurry," Kotler said.

"Glass everywhere," Denzel said, brushing the glass off of the seat with his hand.

They climbed into the car and drove away from the estate. They had already arranged hotel rooms nearby, and would stay there until they could accompany the transfer of the prisoners in the morning. But on the drive to the hotel, they chatted about the night's events.

"What I don't understand is how Gail somehow seems to have a small army of ex-military operatives," Denzel said, shaking his head.

"Her grandfather was in Special Forces," Kotler replied. "If Van Burren really was something of a mentor to Gail, he may be the key to that. He and McCarthy maintained their military connections so that they could entice soldiers into being a part of Van Burren's smuggling operation. That would supply Van Burren with a network of personnel and resources spanning the globe. And Gail has clearly inherited that network."

Denzel nodded. "I've seen things like that. I served with men who went that route, especially after Iraq. But the level of corruption that would take—I know it exists. I just don't want it to."

Kotler understood exactly what he meant. Denzel was, himself, ex-Special Forces. It was like seeing someone in your family turn to a life of crime. He was going to take all of this very personally.

They arrived at their hotel and settled for the evening. No drinks. No chats. They each ordered food directly to their rooms and agreed to meet in the lobby in the morning.

Kotler undressed, showered, and was relaxing in the large, soft chair in one corner of his room, sipping a glass of wine while reading from his iPad. He desperately wanted to take his mind off of all of this for a few hours.

There was a soft knock on the door.

Kotler opened it to discover Gail McCarthy, pointing a small pistol at him, obscured by a coat folded over her arm.

Kotler stood aside and let her in the room.

"I should have expected you," he said.

She let the door close behind her, keeping the gun on Kotler the entire time.

She had cleaned up since he'd last seen her, but her eyes still looked red and swollen, and the skin around her nose was irritated and raw looking. To the casual observer she would look as if she had a very bad cold.

"I should kill you," she said.

"It wouldn't be your first body," Kotler replied.

She raised the pistol, and Kotler prepared himself for the shot. As best he could, at least. He'd been an idiot to open the door without checking—knowing full well that Gail was out there. But he'd made the mistake, and now he would take the consequences.

But she didn't fire.

"I'm leaving," she said. "I have new papers. I have a way out of the country. I'm untraceable. Thanks to Richard's network, I'll disappear forever."

"Are you trying to convince me or yourself," Kotler asked.

"I'm telling you so that you'll tell Roland."

"*Agent Denzel* isn't going to buy that. He's going to hunt you for the rest of your life, if he has to. You need to know that."

She thought for a moment. "He can try."

She backed up to the door, and covered the pistol with her coat.

"Gail," Kotler said, letting real emotion seep into his voice. "Why?"

She looked at him, a strange expression on her face—a mixture of fear and adrenaline, perhaps. She smiled, and it was an oddly incongruous smile. "What a loaded question," she said. "But the short answer is that it's my legacy, and I wanted it."

"It wasn't," Kotler said, shaking his head. "It never was. It never would have been. It belongs to the world. It's a piece of history we've searched for as long as we've known of any hint of it. Edison was wrong to hide it. But you ... everything you and Van Burren did—it's more than criminal. You're villains."

She laughed, and it was a hollow sound. "Every story needs a villain, doesn't it?" She opened the door and turned to leave, but glanced back one more time. "It wasn't all lies, you know. I wasn't just manipulating you. I ... enjoyed spending time with you."

Kotler said nothing, but watched the door close. He picked up his phone and called Denzel, who was out of his room and racing for the lobby in seconds. Gail had clearly arranged her exit beforehand, however. She was gone before Denzel had a chance to get anywhere near her.

EPILOGUE

PARKWOODS CEMETERY, NEW YORK

KOTLER STOOD AMONG DOZENS OF THE BLACK-CLAD friends and family of Dr. Eloi Coelho, listening to a Catholic priest speak of the man's life and accomplishments. There were many tears, though Kotler's own eyes were dry.

He felt a great sadness at the passing of his friend, but he also felt a pressing responsibility for his death. He knew it was Anwar Adham, ultimately, who was to blame. But that knowledge did little to keep Kotler from feeling guilt over his friend's injury and his passing. He had been there when Coelho had been shot, and had been one of the reasons the man had been targeted.

He felt a hand on his shoulder and looked up to see Roland Denzel. They nodded to each other, and stood in silence among the rest of the mourners.

When the service was done, Kotler and Denzel walked side by side to the progression of cars. Kotler had hired a car for the day, but Denzel had driven in. "I see you had your glass replaced," Kotler said quietly, smiling.

"It does make driving on rainy days a little more pleasant," Denzel said.

Kotler chuckled lightly.

They had stopped amidst several large and ancient-looking grave markers and crypts, and Kotler looked outward at a sea of stones nearly identical to these. After a moment he sighed, and smiled. "It all comes down to the grave I guess," Kotler said. "Pretty much everything I do in life brings me back to the dead."

"You're talking professionally, right?" Denzel asked.

"Professionally, personally, what difference does it make?"

"You know that Coelho's death wasn't your fault," Denzel stated. "You were sucked into something beyond your control."

Kotler was about to respond to that with something wry and self-deprecating when he heard a woman's voice from behind him.

"Dan," she said. And Kotler turned to see Evelyn Horelica.

He hadn't seen her since shortly after her rescue, but she looked radiant and beautiful, even in grief. "Evelyn," Kotler said quietly.

"Dr. Horelica," Denzel said, extending his hand. "It's good to see you again."

She took his hand and smiled. "You too, Agent Denzel."

"I'm glad to see you," Kotler said.

She looked at him for a moment, then hugged him, kissing him on the cheek. "I had to come," she said. "But I can't stay."

Kotler nodded. "Of course, I understand. How long will you be in the city?"

"I'm leaving now," she said. "I just flew in for the funeral."

Kotler felt his heart thumping and his throat tightening. He wanted to say something to her that would convince her to stay, but he knew that was all long past. "I'm glad I could see you," he said.

She smiled, and nodded. "You too," she said. "I hear you've been busy."

Kotler shook his head, not wanting the events surrounding Gail or Atlantis to intrude on Coelho's memory. It could hardly be helped. "I've been working," he said, and even to his own ears it sounded lame and empty. "What about you? Last we spoke, you were staying with your parents."

"I'm on my own again now," she said. "I've gotten a new job. I started working as Director of Research with the Alvarez Foundation."

Kotler nodded. "I've heard of it, but haven't had much experience with them. What sort of research do they do?"

"They have various silos, but one of their charters is to look for evidence of ancient diseases and determine any links to modern varietals. Not necessarily my field, but there's quite a bit of translation work to be done. And they needed someone who understood the process of recovering, restoring, and translating ancient texts. It's fascinating."

She smiled when she said this, and Kotler felt a slight bit of relief. He hadn't seen that smile in some time. And then it faded as she looked at him, and her eyes darted away. She still connected him to her ordeal, and she hadn't yet recovered from the experience. He was too much of a reminder of a wound too fresh to bear.

"Well," she said then, "I have to go. I have a flight to catch."

Kotler nodded. "It was good to see you, Evelyn."

She nodded, smiled politely at Denzel, and then turned and walked away.

"And the hits just keep coming," Denzel said.

Kotler looked up at him. Denzel was looking at Kotler

with a worried expression, and Kotler laughed lightly. "Just the way it goes," he said.

"You need scotch," Denzel replied.

And Kotler couldn't have agreed more.

They sat in a bar, reminiscing about Coelho and Evelyn and Vikings. And then the conversation turned inevitably to Gail McCarthy.

"I'm going to find her," Denzel assured him.

"I have no doubt. And I'll help, any way I can."

"I appreciate that. But for now, I think maybe we both move on to something else for a bit. There's more to the world than chasing turncoat debutantes. Which reminds me —I have a check for you."

Kotler laughed. "I appreciate it, but I told you—"

"Yeah, I know, you don't need the money. But rules are rules. Donate it if you want."

"Consider it donated," Kotler nodded.

"So are you going to stick with this?" Denzel asked.

Kotler shook his head. "Stick with what?" he asked.

"Consulting," Denzel said. "Because … well, something's come up."

Kotler looked at him, surprised. "You have another case?"

"Lots of them, as it turns out. We've gotten some attention from Washington. I was pulled into a meeting with several higher ups yesterday, and they proposed something … interesting."

"I'm all ears," Kotler smiled.

"They're considering expanding the charter of White Collar Crimes, creating a special branch that specializes in cases involving historic artifacts. They were impressed by what you and I pulled off with these past two cases. They want me to head a special division—and they want you to be an advisor."

"A special division?"

"They have one for art crimes, but this goes beyond that. Antiquities and historical crimes are something we don't have many resources to deal with. Not directly. Not yet. But there are a number of unsolved cases involving just that sort of thing. And since you and I have a track record ..."

"Two cases represents a track record?" Kotler asked, smiling.

"Two cases back-to-back," Denzel said. "But you've ... well, you have a history of this sort of thing."

Kotler couldn't deny that statement. His past was a jumble of looking into and solving the riddles of out of place history. In many ways, he'd very nearly prepared himself all his life for exactly this type of role.

"It sounds intriguing," Kotler said. "So what are the details? And especially, what parts will I not like?"

"That remains to be seen," Denzel said. "But if you're willing to come in for a follow-up meeting, we can hammer out the details. Are you interested?"

Kotler sipped his scotch and thought for a moment.

If all of the events of his life had prepared him for anything, it was this sort of work. He had enjoyed a life of academia—but publishing what he'd found and discovered in his travels was nearly always met with resistance and scorn from his colleagues. No matter how many discoveries he made or articles he published or books he wrote, Kotler would always be considered an outsider in the field.

Despite being well-liked by many of his colleagues, Kotler also faced challenges from the very people he most admired. And that was fed, most often, by the fact that Kotler's discoveries tended to change everything.

If there was one thing that could be counted on when it came to academics, it was an assured closed-mindedness and a diligent resistance to change. And change was what Kotler was continuously bringing to the field. New perspectives, new interpretations, new ideas and new discoveries.

New history, in effect.

Could he gain more satisfaction, and contribute more to the meaning of his life and to history as a whole, by working with Denzel on these sorts of cases? He had searched for meaning his whole life, in a variety of sciences. Would he find it now in the most unlikely place he could imagine?

"I'm interested," he said, offering his glass for a toast.

Denzel smiled as they clinked glasses. "Good," he said. "Because I already told them you were in."

STUFF AT THE END OF THE BOOK

When I wrote 'The Coelho Medallion,' I included a note at the end that revealed the whole thing as a dare. Nick Thacker, my good friend and fellow author (as well as my occasional writing partner), had put the idea to me more than once, and eventually he had outright dared me to do it. So I did.

And it turned out to be one of the best decisions I ever made.

Turns out, I dig thrillers. I knew that from reading them, of course, and I'd written a few books and stories that I had felt would fit nicely in the thriller category. But 'Coelho Medallion' was the very first full-on, no-frills thriller I'd ever decided to pen. And while working on it, I had so much fun and got so much out of it, I was pretty well hooked. It may not be the only genre I write in for the rest of my career, but I'm more than a little proud of the work I'm doing in it.

From that first book, I had created a set of characters that I thought I could really have some fun with. And so almost before I'd put that last period on the page, I had already decided I wanted to write more Dan Kotler stories. Which was a big part of what prompted me to start 'The Atlantis Riddle.'

Now it's time for a confession: This book, too, has an inside joke.

Way back before I'd ever even considered the story of 'Coelho Medallion,' Nick Thacker wrote a book set in A.G. Riddle's "Origin Mystery" universe—the most famous of which was Riddle's first book, 'The Atlantis Gene.'

Nick's book, 'The Atlantis Deception,' was a short and fast-paced read that was essentially 'Jurassic Park in Space,' and I had the honor and privilege of being the first one to read it. I read it overnight, offered notes and tweaks, and within a few days it was available for download on Amazon.com.

Nick had high hopes for the book, and so did I. But it prompted a conversation in which I said, "We should totally write a book called 'The Atlantis Riddle,' and see if we can pick up some of A.G. Riddle's readers just based on the title!"

It was a joke, and man, did we laugh. But it was also kind of a neat idea—the irony of it, the sort of game of it, appealed to both of us. But it was a thriller, clearly. It had to be. Maybe there could be a bit of scifi in it, but it was a thriller at heart—and I didn't write thrillers.

Until, one day, I did.

The first Dan Kotler book has several inside jokes, but one of them is the name itself. The book is named for Paulo Coelho, the amazing and brilliant author who brought 'The Alchemist' into the world. Coelho is a man of calm wisdom, and 'The Alchemist' is a life-changing book that exudes spirituality and a connection to the divine.

So in part, my book is meant to be an homage to Coelho, whose name was both exotic enough to suit the tone of my book and also recognizable by a few, who might just give the book a chance based on the name alone. It is, however, difficult to spell and pronounce, for many. But I can live with that.

The character of Eloi Coelho was, of course, based partially on Paul Coelho. Not much, honestly, but enough. I wanted to capture some of the real Coelho's sensitivity and wisdom, but my Coelho studies humanity in a dramatically different way, mostly through its ruin and what it has left behind.

Nothing should be made of the fact that my Coelho died due to complications from a gunshot wound. I wrote that into 'Atlantis Riddle' for a variety of reasons, none of which imply any ill will toward one of my favorite authors.

In a sense, 'Atlantis Riddle' is more than just a sequel to 'Coelho Medallion.' It's a final few chapters in that tale. Because even though Kotler and Denzel go off on another grand adventure together, there were still threads connecting them to the events of the first book. There were open loops I felt had to be addressed. And, of course, I created new open loops in the process. So you can figure there will be more of these books in the future.

What I wanted to do with Dan Kotler is open up a way of looking at the world that's both exciting and a bit different. I wanted a character who was at once a part of the academic and scientific world, but also alienated from it. I wanted someone who was nearly super heroic in terms of his intelligence, but was still vulnerable to the same emotions and weaknesses we all share. And I wanted someone who had trained his whole life for a purpose, without fully realizing what that purpose might be.

I think I've struck that balance. You'll have to let me know.

Dan Kotler is an epic character. He's brilliant—with multiple PhDs and in disparate fields of study. He's inventive and clever. He's wry and quick witted. He's essentially everything I ever wanted to be, but I became me instead. Still ... I write the guy. That stuff has to be in here somewhere.

Roland Denzel, on the other hand, was never even on my radar. In fact, I was nearly halfway through 'Coelho Medallion' before I realized that Denzel was the perfect Watson to Kotler's Holmes. Though I'd never tell him that—he'd be just as likely to punch me as to agree. But unlike Watson, Denzel is a leading man in his own right. He's also pretty sharp, though he hides it well sometimes. He's tactical. He's well-tempered. He's aggressive when he has to be, but knows when to hold back. He's ambitious, but only in that he wants to serve more people, better. He's a soldier who is done with battles, but still fights the war.

I'm sorry, but now that I've drawn the Sherlock connection, I'm having a hard time ignoring it. It's clear that was more of an influence than I intended. You've learned it at the same time I've learned it.

But where there is a key difference, to my thinking, is that neither Kotler nor Denzel thinks of the other as inferior in any way. In fact, both seem to have a sort of fascination with each other, and an admiration that goes well beyond friendship and edges into brotherhood. They tease each other. They harass each other. They trust each other with their very lives. Not bad, considering they only met perhaps a year or so ago.

And in that, I now have to consider that Kotler and Denzel may well represent me and Nick Thacker. We met in one of the most casual and clinical ways—I approached him for author coaching as I was figuring out my author career path. We hit it off in that first call, and more calls followed. We teamed up on his podcast (Self Publishing Answers), and shared the burdens and headaches of that. And without meeting each other in person for nearly a year, we became incredibly close friends. He's a brother to me, and I'll swear by that.

We've met in person a few times now, and talked more times than I can count. Our text messages back and forth can border on epic. And we are generally each other's first reader, which works out well for both of us. But in all of this, Nick and I have a dynamic that's very much like the one that plays out between Kotler and Denzel—though I'd be hard pressed to say who is whom in this scenario.

Let's just say that the camaraderie and brotherhood and loyalty of the two comes directly from what Nick and I share. And that could be why the relationship between Kotler and Denzel feels so real. I'm totally stealing it.

All that said and examined, 'The Atlantis Riddle' may have started as yet another inside joke, but it's part of an ever-growing universe of stories that I hope are as inspiring as they may be entertaining. I write them with a sense of pride and joy at telling these tales, and my very sincere hope is that you are reading them with that same feeling.

There will be more Dan Kotler stories. That's a promise. As long as you keep reading them, they will be there. I don't know how many there will be before my time is up on this Earth—maybe one, maybe one hundred. But there will be more.

Thank you for being a part of this discovery about myself, by the way. I appreciate you for reading this far, and I invite you to email me at kevin@tumlinson.net to let me know what you think of this or any of my books.

And if you'd be so kind, and especially if you enjoyed this book, please go and review it on Amazon.com, Goodreads, Apple iBooks, and anywhere else you can.

Thank you, and happy reading.
Kevin Tumlinson
Sugar Land, TX - October 6, 2016

ABOUT THE AUTHOR

Kevin Tumlinson was born in Wild Peach, Texas, in 1972. He spent most of his childhood running barefoot in places no sane human would tread even with boots on. With only three fuzzy channels on television and the invention of game consoles still slightly out of reach, Kevin learned at an early age to keep himself and his family and friends entertained with stories and anecdotes. He did not always tell his family and friends that these were stories or anecdotes.

Kevin has been writing professionally since he was twelve years old, and has an ever-growing library of novels, novellas, and non-fiction books to his credit. He is an award-winning copywriter, and once endured a shockingly long career in marketing, media, and documentary television. He's also a renowned expert on pants jokes, with over a thousand in his repertoire--far greater than the actual number of pants he owns.

Learn more about Kevin and his work on his website, and get three of his best books for free when you register at kevintumlinson.com/starterlibrary

Connect with Kevin:

kevintumlinson.com
kevin@tumlinson.net

HOW TO MAKE AN AUTHOR STUPID GRATEFUL

If you loved this book, and you'd like to see more like it, I can totally help with that. And there are some things you can do that will help *me* help *you*:

(1) REVIEW THIS BOOK

Go to Amazon, Goodreads, Apple's iBooks Store and anywhere else you can think of and leave a review for this book. Seriously—**I can't tell you enough how much this helps!**

The more reviews a book has, the more discoverable it becomes. Help me build and grow an audience for the books so I can keep writing and publishing them!

(2) BECOME A SLINGER

Slingers are what I call the people who are on my mailing list. They get the latest updates on new book releases, blog posts, podcast episodes, and (coolest of all) FREE GIVEAWAYS.

Best of all, if you sign up, you can get the Kevin Tumlinson Starter Library for FREE.

Go to http://kevintumlinson.com/starterlibrary download your free books now!

(3) TELL YOUR FRIENDS

Without readers, an author is just some guy with a really crappy hobby. Long hours at the keyboard. Tons of money spent on editing, layout, cover design. Even more long hours waiting for reviews and sales and bits of praise on Twitter. Honestly, a fella could take up fishing.

So please, spread the word. If you liked this book, tell a friend. Send them to that link above and let them download some free books. Help me grow this author business, and I promise I'll do everything I can to keep you entertained as much as possible!

Thanks for your help. And thanks for reading.